"And what would come of those changes to my country—all that hard work—if I were to allow my wife to divorce me?" Odir said, just for once allowing free rein to his seething mass of emotions. "All of them would turn to dust should their king divorce his queen."

"You are not king yet, Odir. Although it would be difficult, you can still obtain a divorce before you take the throne."

Eloise's words were little daggers, finding their way into his heart, and Odir cursed the slip of his tongue that might have revealed the extent of the power she held at this very moment.

He fought with the feelings in his chest—all the anger, grief and exhaustion from the last twelve hours. He wielded them like weapons and went on the attack. If her trust fund was the only thing that Eloise was holding out for, he could match that easily.

"Let me go, Odir. Just let me go and you will never have to hear from me again."

From the dark corner of the room a bitter laugh emerged, and he stepped from the shadows into a shaft of moonlight.

"I wish I could. I really do. But sadly I can't. So, I have a deal for you. Return to my side and I will give you two million pounds. Have my child and I will give you five more."

Pippa Roscoe lives in Norfolk near her family and makes daily promises to herself that this is the day she'll leave the computer to take a long walk in the countryside. She can't remember a time when she wasn't dreaming about handsome heroes and innocent heroines. Totally her mother's fault, of course—she gave Pippa her first romance to read at the age of seven! She is inconceivably happy that she gets to share those daydreams with you all. Follow her on Twitter, @PippaRoscoe.

This is Pippa's stunning debut for Harlequin Presents— we hope you enjoy it!

Pippa Roscoe

CONQUERING HIS VIRGIN QUEEN

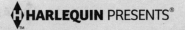

HARLEQUIN PRESENTS®

Recycling programs
for this product may
not exist in your area.

ISBN-13: 978-1-335-41931-6

Conquering His Virgin Queen

First North American publication 2018

Copyright © 2018 by Pippa Roscoe

Printed in U.S.A.

CONQUERING HIS VIRGIN QUEEN

To my mother and sister, who show me each and every day what a true heroine is.

And to Stella, who told me the kindest lie, giving me courage to submit the first (terrible!) draft of this story.

I can't thank you enough.

CHAPTER ONE

August 1st, 20.00-21.00, Heron Tower

TO SAY THAT Odir Farouk Al Arkrin, twelfth genera-
tion Farrehed warrior, eldest son of Sheikh Abbas
and leading world business figure, was having a bad
day would be a dramatic understatement. The Prince
pulled the loops of his English-style bowtie together,
shaking off the feeling of a noose closing around his
neck, and bit back a curse. A curse that damned the
wife he had not seen for six months.

But his past feelings about her didn't matter. Her
recent absence didn't matter.

Within an hour she would return to him.

And he'd get what he needed—what his *country* needed.

Odir pulled the edges of the black silk fabric
tight, firmly fixing the tie in place. Stepping back,
he checked his image in the full-length mirror. The
sun, setting over the London skyline, caught in the
reflection of the mirror and briefly stung his eyes be-

fore dipping behind his broad shoulders. He tugged at the cuffs of the tailor-made tux that was equally as uncomfortable as his royal robes. Each were trappings, a costume for the role that he was required to play. And tonight, in one of England's most renowned and expensive hotels, he'd play the role of a lifetime.

Behind him stood Malik, his personal bodyguard and a man he'd known since they had both run about the Farrehed palace in little more than nappies. A man who nearly six months before had betrayed him in the most shocking way. Frustration rose up within him, and this time Odir just couldn't hold back.

'Wipe the look of guilt from your face or leave. I can't have you making people curious. Not now.'

Malik opened his mouth to speak, but Odir cut him off.

'And if you don't have the good sense to stop apologising then I will send you back to Farrehed and you can spend the rest of your life guarding my father's sister. And, trust me, that is a promise, not a threat. She eats more than a camel and lives like a tortoise. You will die of boredom before your time, and that would be a waste.'

Malik didn't even twitch. It was the first time Odir had made a joke in what felt like months, and not only had it fallen flat, but a burst of shame cut through him. Now wasn't the time for jokes.

'Are you sure you want to do this?' Malik asked.

Perhaps it was only because Malik was standing behind him that he dared to ask that question. But Odir reluctantly acknowledged that it echoed his own struggling mind.

'Want? No. Am I sure? Yes. It must be done.'

There was a knock on the door and his personal advisor poked his head through the opening, clearly aware of what kind of mood his Prince was in and not daring to enter further into the dark aura that had surrounded Odir since that morning.

'Has the press conference been arranged?' Odir tossed over his shoulder, meeting his aide's curious glance in the mirror.

'Yes, My—'

'Don't. Don't call me that. Not yet.'

'Of course, *Sir*. Yes, the press have been called for eight o'clock tomorrow morning at the embassy. Sir…?'

'Yes?'

'We can still cancel the event tonight.'

'This yearly event has been upheld through two skirmishes, one war, one financial depression and a royal wedding—and that's just in the last thirty years. It's taken months of planning and even if it hadn't we cannot cancel. To do so would be seen as a sign of weakness. And that—right now—is untenable.'

His assistant nodded, but didn't leave, instead hovering on the threshold as if he knew there was something more.

'The invitation…it went out this morning? She received it?'

Another nod.

Once Odir's security team had discovered the fake name his wife was using on her equally fake passport, it hadn't taken them more than thirty minutes to track down her whereabouts. From there it had been easy for his consulate in Switzerland to deliver the invitation to her address. An address he'd never visited nor known about until ten hours ago.

'You can go,' he said, and his assistant disappeared back through the door.

Odir returned his focus to the mirror, and although a part of him wanted to close his eyes against the white printout lying on the small side table beside his bed, he forced them to remain open. Forced his gaze to scan the blurry photocopy of a passport with a face he recognised bearing a name he didn't. The document had become the physical manifestation of his wife's deceit and he resisted the urge to ball it up and throw it aside.

But that wasn't what had sent a ripple of discord through his body. It was the black and white picture of the woman he had married and vowed before God to honour above all else. And he had, he thought with an arrow of anger. But *she* hadn't.

After six months of seemingly fruitless investigations trying to track down his errant wife, the fact that Malik had seen sense—only in the direst of circumstances—to reveal the name on her fake passport had briefly made Odir wonder whether Eloise had put Malik under some kind of wicked spell too. But he'd discarded the thought as quickly as it had come. Malik would never have touched his wife. Only one other had, and no matter how angry, how furious he was, he couldn't and wouldn't harm a hair on that body.

Another glance at the black and white photocopy, lying on the depressingly thin file of information his security team had dug up on her, creased and limp already from heavy fingers and angry hands, spiked his frustration once again.

His wife had always been beautiful. A beauty that had once threatened to undo him. But that wasn't what he was looking for. Odir wanted to know if she had been blushing with shame when that photograph was taken. But the soft white planes of her face set against the grey shadow of her hair told him nothing.

Odir ruthlessly forced away the frustration welling in his chest. He didn't have time to give in to such base things. He never had.

Tonight he had but one goal.

'You have confirmation of her arrival?' he threw at Malik.

'She landed at Gatwick five hours ago.'

A curl of tension loosened its grip on him. Everything was falling into place.

'She was followed to a hotel in London where

she spent two hours, made a few phone calls,' Malik continued. 'She left in a cab and should arrive here in twenty minutes.'

Odir wondered why Eloise hadn't fled to her family's posting in Kuwait. He knew that she didn't get on with her father. There had always been a strange, unsettling and silent bond between the young woman who had followed her ambassador father to Farrehed after finishing her university studies. A father who hadn't noticed his daughter had been missing for six months. Hell, *he* hadn't even noticed for three whole days.

But his lack of knowledge about her family was just another sign that he should have known more about the woman he'd bound himself to. He'd believed his father when he'd said their marriage would be good for his country. Would cement much-needed ties between their desert kingdom and Britain. And, although Odir had been brought up to expect an arranged marriage, what he'd found when he'd met Eloise two years ago had given him hope. Hope that he'd have a chance at finding something true—something more. Instead he'd been blinded by lust and what he now considered an award-worthy performance.

Not that it mattered at all. For his wife was going to return to his side no matter what he had to do to ensure it. She had no choice, *he* had no choice, and nothing angered him more than having his hand forced.

'Take your men and meet her in Reception.'

* * *

'Could you pull up around the corner?'

The last thing Eloise wanted was for the Princess of Farrehed to be seen getting out of a local cab right outside the Heron Tower, where her husband's glamorous charity event was being held.

She hadn't seen the tower since it had been built, and the tall glass structure, reaching into the night sky, struck her as an appropriate symbol to represent the power of the husband she hadn't seen in half a year.

A finger of fear trailed its icy tip down the length of her spine and she straightened her shoulders to try and dislodge its hold. Eloise didn't need to know how Odir had found her. In reality, she was actually a little surprised that Malik hadn't told him earlier.

In those first few months the only thing that had distracted her from the belief that Odir would arrive in Zurich and drag her back to Farrehed had been Natalia. Her university friend who, within a matter of days, had thrown Eloise's problems into stark relief.

One day she might look back kindly on the girl who had arrived in Zurich looking over her shoulder, broken by misunderstandings and deeper hurts. But in contrast to Natalia's situation, the Eloise that first came to Switzerland simply looked foolish and spoilt.

Taking a deep breath, Eloise pushed those thoughts aside and tried to focus on the present. What was it her husband wanted? Had he come to the decision that it was time to end their marriage? Or was there a reason that her husband's summons coincided with her birthday tomorrow? The same day that she would finally be able to access the trust fund her grandfather had so kindly and generously secured for her. Surely just a coincidence.

And if she told herself that one hundred times more, perhaps she would start to believe it.

Eloise fingered the embossed invitation that had arrived, hand-delivered, that morning. She had opened the door with her coffee in one hand and accepted the envelope with the other. Looking back, she could hardly credit that it had been only eight hours ago. Nothing had sprung her into action like that demand from her husband to attend tonight's charity event. Nothing. Not even Natalia's illness, her father's blackmail or her mother's indifference.

It had taken her an hour to think out her options, to call the hospital and make arrangements to cover her absence. She could have stayed in Zurich. She could have run again. But if Odir had found her then he knew the name on her fake passport, and without help from Malik she couldn't easily procure another one.

But through all these considerations was the realisation that she should make use of this unexpected summons… and finally put into motion the one thing she'd wanted for the last six months.

Eloise twisted the royal wedding ring around her finger. The weight she'd lost in recent months had

made the fitting loose, and she couldn't help but wonder if it was a sign. A sign that perhaps she was finally about to escape the noose that had been placed
around her neck the moment her ambitious father
had finally got what he wanted as two little words
fell from her lips... *'I do.'*

A car horn crashed into the night from somewhere
behind the cab. She handed the driver the last of her
English money and got out, carefully picking up the
long skirts of the black silk dress she had bought at
the airport. The halter-neck fitted snugly around her
throat, disguising the need for the expensive jewellery that would be expected from the royal princess
she had supposedly been for the last eight months.
The material clung to her chest like a second skin,
and at her bare back she felt a blast of unusually warm
air for London, which was in the throes of a summer
heatwave. She had spent a fortune on it—almost more
than a month's salary. But it was worth it.

She wasn't naïve enough to go to a State event in
a dress of even half the price. And she wasn't naïve
enough to pick a fight with a prince without armour.

Not when that Prince was her husband.

As soon as Eloise stepped through the doors of the
Heron Tower she was flanked by four men dressed
from head to toe in black. For a moment—just a
moment—she imagined the cold clasps of handcuffs
closing around her wrists, and then discarded the

thought as foolish. Her husband might be infuriated with her, but he would never do anything to risk the reputation of the royal family. She knew that better than most. She looked to their faces and was not surprised to see Malik, the only one of the men actually to meet her eye. No one spoke, though if it was a sign of respect, or shame, she couldn't tell.

As they all entered the lift, the guards barring entry to any of the other guests, she allowed herself to feel a burst of hope that after tonight she might finally be free. Her stomach dropped away as the lift drew them higher and higher, giving her the most spectacular night-time view of London. Multi-coloured lights spread out before her and it was almost enough to take her breath away.

But superimposed over the dramatic vista was her pale, shimmering reflection. Her long blonde hair had not been expertly looped and pinned by stylists who knew what they were doing and charged a fortune. Instead she had done her best in the mirror at the cheap hotel she'd rented for the night. And in her mind the two extremes—the poor hotel and the incredibly rich lavish world of the Heron Tower— summed up the last two years of her life.

The poorer part was so much more valuable to her for its freedom…the richer part coming with a price she could no longer pay.

Drawing to a stop sooner than she'd expected, the lift doors opened onto a room lavishly decorated

with leading members of international society—each
adorned in clothes and jewellery that would rival all
the gold in the Bank of England.

She glanced around the soft-hued room, its delicate lighting clashing painfully with the sounds of
clinking glasses and mind-numbing small talk.

The party, it seemed, had started without her.

With Eloise's first step into the room those standing nearby stopped talking, and all around her a hush
seemed to descend. Many bowed their heads, as if
in respect, but she knew it also served to mask their
gossiping mouths. And she hated it. She always had.
The close attention paid to her and her family before
and even more so after she had married Odir. For just
a moment she wondered whether this was how her
mother felt. Hiding her hurt behind practised smiles.
And then she berated herself. Her husband, for all
his sins, was *nothing* like her father.

'Eloise?' A familiar voice cut through the crowds.

Eloise turned to take in the face of one of the only
friends she could claim from her 'old life', as she
now thought of it.

'Emily, it's good to see you,' she replied, surprised
at the truth of her words, and even more surprised as
Emily drew her into a warm embrace.

'Where have you *been*?' Emily whispered into her
ear. 'It's been ages, El. The rumour mill has had you
locked in the Farrehed palace tower by your domi-
neering husband.'

For just a moment Eloise wanted to tell her friend

everything. Of the joy she'd found helping others, the freedom she'd found in Zurich, the meaning she'd found in such a simple existence…

'Mrs Santos,' Malik said, interrupting Eloise's thoughts and putting an end to such a foolish whim.

Of *course* she couldn't say anything that would reveal her absence from Farrehed…from the Prince.

'Malik.' Emily nodded in warm welcome.

'It's a long story,' Eloise replied quietly, with a smile to soften the brush-off. 'What are you doing here? You're not usually at these events.'

'I could say the same for *you*,' the brunette replied in hushed tones. 'My father… He's… He's not doing so well.'

'I'm sorry to hear that. And your husband?'

'Not here—thankfully,' Emily replied with a rueful laugh. 'Speaking of husbands… Yours has been like a bear with a sore head all evening.'

'Really?' Eloise asked, her heart pounding just at the thought of him.

Emily nodded over her shoulder.

And, as if their discussion had conjured his presence, Eloise caught sight of the man she hadn't seen in six months. She couldn't see his face, but the broad lines of his back were etched in her memory as if it were the only way she had ever seen her husband: from a distance and from behind.

Even today he stood a head taller than all those around him, and for one second her breath caught in her lungs. A thousand images of her handsome husband ran through her mind and over her skin. That first ever sight of him, dismounting a formidable black stallion. His impenetrable air of authority before she'd even known he was the son of a sheikh. The way that she had mocked him for his arrogance as he'd flung the horse's reins at the stable hand and the innocent flirtation they had shared—until later that evening when they had been formally introduced.

Betraying nothing of their first meeting, Odir had eased her humiliation, charmed away her embarrassment and made it a secret shared between them, kept from their fathers. One she'd foolishly cherished.

Images crashed through her mind of the brief time they had spent together during their arranged engagement—the trips he'd made out to the borders of Farrehed, where she had been working for a charity set up to help provide medication for the desert tribes. The secret dinners they had shared…the morning they'd watched the sun rise over the sand dunes…

She thought back with shame of how she had told him her hopes and dreams…how she'd eagerly eaten up his plans for Farrehed and its people. Of how they'd come together, in spite of their fathers' plans, to try and make the best of the arrangement. Of how she'd dared to hope that their marriage could be something more.

But it hadn't been. She was a bought bride—a pawn used by powerful men.

Her wedding ring slipped down her finger again. She was done waiting for her prince to come along and rescue her. It was time for the Princess to rescue *herself*.

Odir's cheeks ached from fake smiles, his throat hurt from obsequious small talk and his head pounded from the pressure he'd been keeping at bay all day. He rubbed away the exhaustion from his neck. He'd been through worse, he assured himself, but then wondered whether that was actually true.

At that moment, he would have given half of his country away for a whisky.

But the ruler of Farrehed couldn't be so uncouth as to drink whisky at an event where only the finest champagne was being guzzled by the gallon.

Odir had never quite understood why it required the spending of such large sums of money to raise even greater sums of money for charity. But then the law of diminishing returns was something he'd never held to.

'And that was when she said that she couldn't *see* it!'

Odir joined in the over-zealous laughter at the undeserving joke told by the French Ambassador. And then, instead of turning away and seeking the solitude he so badly wanted, Odir slipped into the kind of seasoned small talk that he could do in his sleep. Perhaps in the brief, heady days of his youth he *had* even done it in his sleep. But that had been before. Before his marriage, before his father's grief-stricken deterioration had signalled the near absolute destruction of his beloved country, and before this morning.

And now, despite all this spectacle, all this civility, the future of Farrehed was hanging by a thread. And the only person who could help him hold on to it was the woman he'd let into his palace to wear his ring.

Behind him Odir felt rather than heard a lull in the conversation and the hairs lifted on his arms. She should never have been able to elicit such a reaction in him. He'd once thought the barriers around his heart strong enough to prevent such a thing. But she had. And she still did.

Eloise—his wife, his future Queen—had arrived.

Odir watched her reflection in the glass as she made her way through the throng of people between them. The closer she got, the more eagerly he ate up the defiance that shone from the angle of her shoulders, her determined footsteps. *Good.* He wanted the promise of the fight she was offering him. He needed it.

He let her get almost within touching distance and then he struck.

Odir wheeled round and imprisoned her within his arms, proceeding to kiss her in a way that he had allowed himself on only a few occasions during their courtship. He took full advantage of her lips, opened partially in shock, and plunged his tongue into…

Into a heaven he'd refused to let himself remember.

As his lips carved out his domination over her he cursed inwardly. The taste of her tongue was shocking in its sweetness, her soft lips taking in every sweep of his firm command. He had meant the kiss to be retribution. He had not for one minute thought that it would be his own punishment. His entire body was on fire, and he jerked back away from her before he could get burnt.

For just a second the shock that lit her features was echoed in his eyes. Only once had he ever felt this way. On their wedding night… It had been a glimpse into the madness that might consume him whole, might tempt him to turn his back on his country's needs.

And then he remembered what had happened two months after their wedding night…the lies and the betrayal… It was enough to return his presence of mind to what had to be done.

'Eloise, *habibti*, I'm sorry. I couldn't help myself,' he said, with a smile so sickly sweet he wondered that anyone could believe it. 'Even two days apart feels like…*months*,' he said, through lips that still held the taste of her.

For a moment he almost hoped that she might slip up, that the hesitation he saw in her eyes would reveal her to be the fraud she truly was, but her instant reply was flawless.

'I'm sorry that I couldn't be on the same flight as you, darling.'

The lie slipped seamlessly from her lips, and yet again he wondered how he'd failed to notice such great skill in her throughout the months of their engagement and their brief marriage. Never mind. He would use it to his advantage and remember not to underestimate her. After all, she had managed to coerce his most loyal personal guard into doing her bidding.

No, it would not pay to underestimate his wife.

That kiss might have stolen her breath, and taunted her with memories of their wedding night—and it certainly was not the welcome that she'd expected from her husband—but that didn't change a thing.

Eloise pushed down the betraying grip of desire that had dusted her body and forced it away before it could take hold. If her will hadn't been enough, then the barely concealed warning in Odir's eyes certainly was.

She had been here before. She had played many roles in her life and played them well. The perfect daughter, the doting wife... Just for one more night she could do it.

Eloise was skilled at recognising illusions and half-truths, but she could almost believe there had been a time when there was more to her husband's glance than cold acceptance.

The French Ambassador claimed her attention with a bow.

'*Ma chère* Eloise—I can't tell you how sorry we were not to see you at the Hanley Cup in May. Matilde and I were just saying so, weren't we?' he asked of his wife.

Glancing at Matilde's avaricious gaze, Eloise knew exactly what kind of speculation they had been involved in, and clearly they were greedily about to eat up the first juicy bit of gossip on Farrehed's errant Princess.

Eloise was prepared to launch into the carefully constructed cover story of her actions over the last months when Odir cut in with an impossibly gentle chuckle. *Chuckle?* She didn't think she'd ever heard such a sound from his lips in all the time she had known him.

'You must forgive my wife. She's been so preoccupied with her *charitable works*—' the heavily laden words for her benefit alone '—that it feels as if I have hardly seen her once in the last six months.'

Matilde's hungry gaze turned into one of reproach, and that only angered Eloise even more. The last words Odir had hurled at her across a room had been so full of fury they had driven her from Farrehed. He had forced her out of her country, her home, and he had the gall to blame *her*?

'Odir, don't exaggerate,' she said playfully, putting a bit more weight than necessary behind a not-so-playful tap on his arm. 'You know *exactly* where I have been.' She turned to Matilde with the most ingratiating smile she had ever given and continued, 'I have been overseeing a project to bring sovereign-funded, mental and medical health care to women of the tribes at the outer reaches of Farrehed.'

It was as close to the truth of what she had been helping to do in Zurich as it could be. As she well knew, the best lies were born from threads of truth. She had learnt that from her mother and father.

'It's no wonder you're here, then,' replied the smiling ambassador's wife, and for a moment, Eloise was confused.

She had been so preoccupied with her husband's summons she hadn't even noticed which of Odir's causes this event was for.

'Eloise would never miss a charitable event that reaffirms the links between the World Health Organisation and the betterment of women in our country. But I hope that you will excuse us,' he said, placing a reassuring hand on the ambassador's shoulder. 'It's a little-known secret that it's my wife's birthday tomorrow, and I have a *special* present for her.'

Odir wrapped his strong arm around her waist like a steel clamp and started manoeuvring her from the room.

'There's only one birthday present I want from you, *darling*, and that's a divorce.'

CHAPTER TWO

August 1st, 21.00-22.00, Heron Tower

'KEEP YOUR VOICE DOWN,' he commanded, pulling her tighter into his side as if he feared that she would try to escape.

Perhaps it wasn't such a silly fear, as from the moment he had put his lips to hers, brushed the inside of her mouth with his tongue, all she'd wanted to do was run.

How galling it was to realise that within seconds of his kiss all she had wanted to do was give herself over to the feelings that she'd been wrong to think had died. Everything in her had surged up, almost bringing her arms to hang on to the lapels of his tux jacket.

People parted before them like the sea, and she knew that they would still have done the same even had he not been a prince, such was the power and authority he wore around him like a protective cloak.

From halfway across the room she could see

Odir's personal guard beginning to gather around a small doorway that led off to the side of the room.

'Where are you taking me, Odir?'

'What? No *darling* for me this time?'

She tried to pull her arm free, but he only tightened his hold.

'Stop it or you'll make a scene. And, as bad a job as you've already been doing as my wife for the last six months, believe me, you don't want to make it worse.'

His response confused her momentarily. What did *he* care if she wasn't being the perfect wife? He certainly hadn't in the two months following their wedding day, having disappeared for weeks on end, leaving her to haunt the halls of the palace alone and lost. Surely the only reason he'd called her to London this evening was because he wanted to sever all ties with her?

Eloise couldn't imagine for one moment that it would be anything else after the last words he'd said to her in Farrehed. After what he believed her to have done.

'*I'm* not the one causing the scene, Odir. You are. I'll ask again. Where are you taking me?'

He seemed to flinch as her voice had become almost loud enough for those closest to them to hear.

'Somewhere we can talk. That *is* what you want, no? To talk?'

'What I want is a—'

He wheeled her around so that she stood in front of him, impossibly close. He leaned in with what would look to the world like the satisfied smile of a loving husband. His lips were just beneath her ear, tantalisingly close.

'Do. Not. Say. That. Again.'

Each whispered word pressed a puff of air against her heated skin, causing her pulse to jump erratically in response—her body seemingly ignorant of the threat his words implied.

He brought her back round to his side and pushed her through the crowd towards a private elevator. The doors slid open without a sound and Eloise stepped into a mirror-lined lift. If he wanted to talk, so be it—as long as it brought about her freedom.

It took her a moment to realise that she was alone with her husband for the first time since their wedding night. Since he had left her by herself, unable to get out of that ridiculous white dress. Standing by his side now, she looked at their reflection, multiplied over and over again until it was all she could see.

She took in the changes that six months had brought to his handsome features. The fine dusting of grey at his temples, shining bright against his thick dark hair. The lines that framed his eyes—closed now—and the hollows beneath his cheekbones, serving only to make him seem even more powerful and commanding. His cologne infused the air about them until it was all she could smell, overwhelming her completely.

She had expected anger from him. Fury, even. Not this cold carelessness that seemed to vibrate from his being. But she was astute enough to recognise the anticipation of anger as a learning from her child-hood. From the powerful men she had encountered. Like her father. Like his.

'Odir—'

'Not yet,' he said, without even bothering to open his eyes.

And all the anger she'd held at bay since the moment his lips had touched hers raised its ugly head and forced its way out.

'No, you'll listen to—'

But before she could finish her sentence the lift arrived at its destination and Odir stalked out into a corridor and through a door being held open by the guard already stationed there.

Eloise followed, feelings of uncertainty and a hatred of being ignored filling her, propelling her forward as she stepped over the threshold of a room she hadn't expected.

Floor-to-ceiling windows launched her gaze out to the London she had glimpsed earlier from the lift. Spread out before them like a blanket made of black silk and sequins, its tiny lights shifted and flashed, outlining the London Eye and the Houses of Parliament. And strangely she felt an ache of homesickness pulse within her, even though she had not lived in London since she'd left university and made her way to Farrehed.

Not even three years later here she was, surveying it as if she were its lord and master.

And then she realised how foolish that thought was. She had never been lord and master of anything. That had been the role of her father and then her husband. The women in her family had never had the privilege of holding such power. Not until she had left her husband's side.

Odir was standing two feet in front of her, but the reflection in the glass distorted the distance between them, showing them as almost side by side. He made no move to turn on the lights in the apartment and shadows swept around them as the clouds sped their way across the light of the moon, casting her husband's face into half-light and shade as he turned to face her.

They might not have shared a bed, and they might not have spoken in half a year, but Eloise knew her husband. Knew that she should not push him. But she couldn't back down now. It had taken everything she had to come here tonight. To face him one last time.

'I want a divorce.'

'What? No small-talk?'

'You want small-talk? Fine. Hello, Husband, how was your day?' she replied, mock sweetness dripping from her voice.

'Pretty bad, actually. How was yours?'

'Equally so, having been summoned halfway across Europe for God knows what reason.'

'I've seen quite a number of sides to you, Eloise.

Sweet and innocent, cold and indifferent. But I think this—righteous indignation—suits you the best.'

Yet he'd never seen the truth of her, she realised. Perhaps he hadn't wanted or needed to once he'd had his ring on her finger. She sighed heavily. This was getting them nowhere.

'Odir. Please. I want a divorce.'

'As you keep saying,' he replied. 'But I'm afraid that doesn't fit with my plans.'

'And *I'm* afraid your plans no longer matter to me. I have built a life for myself in Switzerland. A life that doesn't involve you. I've…changed, Odir. I am not the same woman you married.'

His eyes narrowed at that. Justifiably so. Six months ago she wouldn't even have thought to fight back. But she was now.

'Mmm…' he murmured. 'Perhaps you *have* changed.'

Odir took in the defiance that filled her slim frame. She had lost weight in the last six months, and he wasn't sure that he liked it. He let arrogance fuel his gaze as it dropped to her feet and leisurely made its way back up, over her hips to her breasts, to her face. A gaze that heated her cheeks and stoked a fire within him.

He ate up the subtle changes in her—the way that anger brightened her eyes and flushed her cheeks—and for a second he thought he might possibly be forgiven for mistaking it as arousal. He cursed the way his body reacted, but knew it served as a reminder to be on his guard.

'If you had liked what you saw when we were married, Odir, we might not be in this situation now.'

The barb hit home. It struck at the weakness he'd had for his wife—the one thing he'd promised himself he would not indulge in. Hadn't his father's obsessional love for his wife nearly destroyed his country? Hadn't the impossible attraction between Odir and Eloise nearly made him do the same?

'Don't you *dare* turn this around on me.' His low, dark tone buzzed in the air between them. '*I* may not have graced your bed, but someone else—'

'Stop!'

She issued the command with such force her hand came up between them. And, bastard that he was, he relished her anger. Relished the fact that her feelings matched his own.

'You never did like hearing the truth, did you, Eloise? Always running...always hiding.'

As the words fell from his lips he briefly wondered if they should instead be aimed at himself.

'And *you* were never interested in the truth, Odir. Only in what suited you and Farrehed.'

'What version of the truth would that be, Eloise? I'm curious. Because I'd like to know what I would find on the divorce papers. Would you place the blame at my feet, or would you own the fact that it was you who betrayed me? Tell me, Eloise, would you be ready to see, splashed all over the pages of the international press, the fact that you committed adultery with *my brother*?'

Eloise wanted to scream. Her hands were clenched into fists and she knew that her nails would leave crescent-moon-shaped indentations in her palms, but still she couldn't release them. Because if she did they would be hurled against her husband, and she didn't know if she would be able to stop.

Never had he asked her for the truth of that night. Not once.

'Get out! Get out of my sight and don't you dare come back!'

The words rang through her mind and she felt her heart break twice over—once for the past and once for the present. Odir had made an assumption. The wrong one. And he had never looked back, using it instead as an excuse to avoid his bought bride.

The night Odir had found his brother trying to kiss her had been one of the worst of her life. He hadn't given either her or his brother the chance to explain. And clearly Jarhan had never put him right. Then again, she hadn't really expected him to.

She tried to shake off the memory of Jarhan's drunken attempts to kiss her but its hold was too great and it dragged her under.

She was in a different room…in a different country. She had been keeping Jarhan company ever since Sheikh Abbas had unveiled his plans for his younger son to wed the Princess of a nearby principality— Kalaran. She had been trying to comfort him, trying to convince him to explain, to tell the truth. But the fear in Jarhan's eyes had been very real.

Stains from the red wine he'd been drinking all night had scored red grooves into the corners of his mouth, and the second his thin lips had crashed painfully against hers the young Prince had gone from being someone she had considered a friend and confidant to becoming the weapon of her undoing.

It was a kiss that had broken a marriage, a brotherhood, and the tentative future she had hoped one day to have.

'So you still won't believe me.'

'Believe *what*? More lies from that delicious mouth of yours?'

The scorn in his words was completely at odds with the compliment he had given away so easily. He turned away and she let out a breath so heavy with grief it surprised even herself.

There had been a time, she acknowledged, when she'd cherished the idea of marrying Odir. Back then, barely two years ago, she had thought even the sun couldn't shine brighter than Odir. He'd charmed her with a self-deprecation and a quick, warm wit she hadn't expected. For a year during their engagement she had watched him, studied the care with which he spoke to palace attendants, seen his love of his people enter every decision he made, every act he chose.

He had been her childhood fantasy come to life. What had started out as their fathers' business agreement had been moulded—so she had thought—by *them*. Together they had made something of their advantageous union. A friendship, she had once thought. A relationship, she had once hoped.

Here was the Prince who would whisk her away from the pains of her childhood—the Prince who would break the hold her father had over her. She had thought that perhaps he might even be her confidant— that finally she would have someone on her side.

But that had been before the reality of her marriage had struck, and all of Odir's words and promises had disappeared into lonely nights as he'd found excuse after excuse to avoid her at every turn, leaving her cold and alone.

Now Eloise sought Odir amongst the shadows and could see determination painted across those features she had once longed to see soften and show something close to the love that they were reported to feel for each other. Looking at him now, she realised that she had been a child, with childish dreams.

She knew then that there was nothing she could say—no defence she could make of that night or any of the nights from then to now. Nothing would make any difference.

'The past isn't going to change. But the future can.'

His grim smile infuriated her.

'You can say it as many times as you like, Eloise. It's not going to happen.'

'Odir, please. See reason. There was once a time when we could talk openly…' She hated the longing that had crept into her voice. 'Don't you *want* to move on? Don't you *want* to find a suitable princess? One who will be the right person to rule by your side one day and provide you with…with the heirs you need?'

She hoped that he would be swayed by the practicality of her argument—the same kind of practicality that had always defined their relationship.

Until she met his eyes. And then she knew that she was just as foolish as that girl who had once hoped this man would rescue her like one of the knights of old and whisk her away to a magical kingdom…

'So, with your birthday tomorrow, on the brink of inheriting what I have been told is your grandfather's considerable trust fund, you're finally ready to ask for a divorce?'

The accusation heavy in his words was bad enough, but the fact that he knew about her grandfather's trust fund was a shock.

'How do you know about that?'

'It's amazing what investigators can find out in only the briefest of hours.'

How she wished she could make him understand

about her trust fund—wished she could tell him what she wanted to do with the money. How she wanted to use it to help Natalia get the treatment she so desperately needed—the only way to treat the painful medical condition that would one day end her life before it had really ever begun.

But before she could create a response his furious words continued.

'Tell me honestly, were you only waiting until your trust fund was released before you came to me asking for a divorce?'

She couldn't deny it. Couldn't deny that she'd had no other option. Her father's machinations meant that until she had access to her trust fund she couldn't leave this marriage. And she couldn't explain to her husband why.

'Were you always such a gold-digger? Or did a taste of royal life—even as brief as it was—ignite such an obscene fire for wealth in you?'

He hated the words that had exploded into the room, called forth from his deeply held anger. They burnt his tongue and scoured his throat, as if punishing him for the cruel taunt.

'If that's what you think of me then we *really* need a divorce, Odir. It's impossible to have two people bound together with such...*hatred*.'

'You made vows before God—before my country's King and before its people. We don't have a choice.'

'There's *always* a choice. I've seen the changes you've made in your country in the last six months. You've done incredible things. Things that have done so much to restore global respect for Farrehed.'

Could he hear admiration in her voice? It surprised him that she had kept up with the changes he'd had to make in the last months. The gruelling hours he'd spent undoing the destruction his father had caused. Or was it just carefully designed research in order to bolster her argument and get what she wanted?

He wondered what it would take for her to realise that what *she* wanted didn't matter. That what *he* wanted didn't matter. Not now. Not after…

He shut down the direction of his thoughts before they could take hold. He couldn't afford to think about it. Not now. After he had her agreement, maybe. And maybe, even then, not until after the press conference.

He forced his mind back to their conversation.

'And what would come of those changes—all that hard work—if I were to allow my wife to divorce me? Now that I have dragged Farrehed kicking and screaming into the twenty-first century? Now that I have ploughed money, time and energy into investments that will make Farrehed a global economy? One that survives—no, *flourishes*—in spite of the current climate? I'll tell you what would come of those changes, Eloise,' he said, just for once allowing free rein to his seething mass of emotions. 'All of them would turn to dust should their King divorce his Queen.'

'You are not King yet, Odir. Although it would be difficult, you can still obtain a divorce before you take the throne.'

Her words were little daggers, finding their way into his heart, and Odir cursed the slip of his tongue that might have revealed the extent of the power she held at this very moment.

He fought with the feelings in his chest…all the anger, grief and exhaustion from the last twelve hours. He wielded them like weapons and went on the attack. If her trust fund was the only thing that Eloise was holding out for, he could match that easily.

'Let me go, Odir. Just let me go and you will never have to hear from me again.'

From a dark corner of the room a bitter laugh emerged, and he stepped from the shadows into a shaft of moonlight.

'I wish I could. I really do. But sadly I can't. So, if money is your only motivating factor, then I have a deal for you—one that will exceed your grandfather's trust fund. Return to my side and I will give you two million pounds. Have my child and I will give you five more.'

CHAPTER THREE

August 1st, 22.00-23.00, Heron Tower

ELOISE COULDN'T QUITE believe she'd heard him correctly, only just resisting the urge to shake her head and dislodge the imaginary blocking of her ears.

He wanted her to do...*what?*

Was this some kind of sick joke?

But the grim look of determination painted across Odir's features spoke volumes.

Her mind raced, working through each of the different possibilities at lightning speed, and the quicker it went the sicker she felt with each passing second. The amount of money was obscene, and certainly more than her grandfather's trust fund. It wouldn't only pay for Natalia's medical bills far into the future, it would allow the medical centre on the brink of closure to move forward and help so many more people.

But she would have to return to Odir's side. She would have to return to Farrehed under the microscope of the world's press. She would never go back to her little Swiss flat, would never see Natalia's happy smile and enjoy her easy companionship. She would never have the freedom of walking alone through the clean, beautiful streets of Zurich. She would have to give up her position as PA to the medical centre's CFO.

Hurt opened up a chasm within her. She loved her job—she liked *working*. Like feeling that she was paying her own way for once in her life and doing something good. And now, just like that, all the possible futures she was considering burnt to ash.

If she were to accept the money—for the centre— she would never be free. She would be required to provide heirs in a marriage built on nothing but lies and distrust. She had grown up the product of such a marriage, and the one vow she'd ever made to herself was that she would never do to a child what had once been done to her.

She looked at Odir and was surprised to find him smiling.

'I can see that you're thinking about it,' he said.

He stalked over to the drinks cabinet and poured himself the whisky he'd wanted earlier that evening. He grimly wondered why he wasn't happier with her consideration of his proposal—why there wasn't a feeling of victory spreading through him. Then he forced his mind ahead a few hours to the international press conference arranged for eight the following morning.

To be standing alone when he made his announcement would make him look weak—would make his *country* look weak—and that was simply untenable.

He felt suddenly as if he were standing on a precipice the size of the Grand Canyon. Farrehed was about to be plunged into a time of great turmoil, and as he looked over at the slip of a woman standing before him, staring at him in horror as if he were the devil, he knew that she alone could ensure its security.

'You can't make such an obscene offer and then stand in silence waiting for a response,' Eloise declared.

She had been watching him closely. She had seen the emotions pass over his distinguished features. Her father had never liked Odir. He'd said it was because he could never tell what the young royal was thinking. But Eloise had never had that problem. Although she couldn't explain why, she had always known what he was thinking. She had before, and she did now.

Despite the obvious distaste he felt about the offer he was making, the belief that he had her agreement had relaxed his frame. She knew that look well. It was the same look her father would get when he knew he was going to get what he wanted.

And she hated it.

Summoning up all her strength, she knew that there was no way she could return to the marriage she had left—no matter what she had once felt for Odir. She was tired of people thinking the worst of her, tired of the sacrifices she had made for people who cared nothing for her, tired of being alone and unwanted.

'I will not take one penny of your money, Odir. I want a divorce and I'll do whatever—*whatever*—it takes to get it.'

'I'll double it,' he replied, as if a total of fourteen million pounds were nothing to him.

She bit back the curse that threatened to fall from her lips. With that much money she could move Natalia and the whole medical facility to Farrehed. She might even be able to convince her mother to come too. The people she loved the most in the world would never want for anything ever again.

Nausea rolled through her as she realised that she was actually considering his offer. Never had she dreamed that there would be anything he could say to make her consider returning to that life—the life she had fled from.

She took a breath and closed her eyes. *Count to ten. Always count to ten before making a decision.*

It was as if the world had stopped turning. He could see it in her eyes. He could see that she was about to say the one word he needed to hear.

And then the tension was broken in an instant with three little knocks on the door. He could have kicked something. *Hard*.

'Enter,' he commanded in a tone that implied nothing of the sort.

His aide peered round the door.

'Your speech, My— *Sir*,' the aide hastily corrected himself. 'It is time.'

Odir cursed out loud and his aide looked shocked. Odir had not realised they had spent so long in the suite. Once again his wife was distracting him from his duty. Just as she had done during their engagement. His preoccupation with her—his determination to forge a kind of relationship that wouldn't replicate his parents'—had spectacularly backfired, and prevented him from seeing the damage his father was doing.

He was going to have to pay more attention. Because he didn't have time for mistakes. He hadn't expected Eloise to jump at his offer, but still… There had been something unsettling about her response. It hadn't quite rung true. If she was just after money there would have been something like victory, like avarice in her eyes… Not what he had seen—what he didn't want to put a name to.

Because if he did it might just undo all his carefully made plans.

Without waiting to see if she would follow, Odir strode from the room and entered the lift. He felt some small satisfaction when Eloise stepped in just behind him and took her place beside him.

The silence between them held all the way back to the function room and Odir used every second of it to curse his father for more things than one, and to curse his own youthful stupidity.

He had agreed to the convenient marriage laid out by both their fathers. A marriage that would benefit all concerned.

But that hadn't been what he'd wanted once he'd met Eloise.

Perhaps it was because they had met before she'd known who he was. That day in the stables. Had she slipped under his defences then? The first woman not to treat him with calculating looks and speculation? She had turned her quick-witted tongue against him, mocked him as no one had done before. Perhaps it was then that his desire for her had flamed brightest—*before* he had discovered his father's wishes and her identity.

Or perhaps it was when he'd thought he'd seen the relief in her eyes as he'd approached her with *his* offer. One that would welcome a relationship between them.

He'd wanted his future to be more than a cold arrangement but less of an intense obsession such as his father had felt for his mother. He'd thought the practicality of that would safeguard him.

But he'd been wrong.

The evening of his wedding the kiss they'd shared had been incendiary. One he'd so desperately wanted to explore that when his aide had approached him, panicked with the news that might throw Farrehed into war, Odir had paused.

For one moment he'd actually considered letting the world go to hell, because all he'd wanted was to lose himself in his new bride. To luxuriate in the sensual promise still heavy on his tongue from her lips.

And in that horrible moment he'd known the madness his father had felt for his mother.

The fact that his father had used his son's wedding day to disguise his invasion into Terhren was unspeakable. But the greater betrayal was Odir's, because he should have known better.

So he'd left his bride waiting for him in his palace suite and taken a helicopter with a handful of aides, leaving the rest to follow the next day. And he had embarked on three weeks of intense, secret negotiations with the Sheikh of Terhren.

And when he'd returned? He'd done everything in his power to shake the hold of their attraction. To ensure that he would never be tempted to disregard his duty again. He'd thrown himself into trade negotiations, soothing the effects of his father's hurts and betrayals, and developed the infrastructure that would make Farrehed great again.

And now, to ensure that all that work, all his sacrifice, wouldn't crumble to dust come eight tomorrow morning, he needed his wife's agreement to return to his side.

He would have her answer before he gave the speech. And if she still said no? Well, then he had his next weapon at hand—one that she wouldn't be able to shake off.

The noise that greeted them as they exited the lift was deafening and disorientating.

The events of the last hour had gone to her head. Odir's offer, delivered in the form of an uncompromising command, still pounded in Eloise's head, mixing with the painful cacophony of hundreds of inebriated conversations.

It was a shock to the system for a woman who had been living such a quiet, modest and almost unrecognisable life for the last six months.

Each and every one of them would stop and stare if they knew that the future Sheikha of Farrehed had been working as a personal assistant to the CFO of a private medical facility, tucked away in the heart of Zurich.

Eloise's heart ached. She missed the calm practicality and sensible comfort of her life there. It hurt to step back into this world of deceitful smiles, barbed compliments and cutting remarks, all hidden beneath a light tone as if laughter would make such inherent rudeness socially acceptable.

She looked about her and saw it all dressed up

in diamonds as if they would hide the dirt. And she wondered for perhaps the first time what would happen if she let her poised façade drop and allowed her true self out…

Odir nearly groaned out loud as the young Prince of Kalaran marched towards them with a sneer painted across his fleshy features.

'Odir,' he said, barely veiling his contempt, and then turned to Eloise. 'Oh, I don't think we've met?'

Fury ignited in Odir and protective instincts danced across his hackles. It was one thing for *him* to take issue with his wife, but something completely other for the Prince of Kalaran to be so openly disrespectful to the future Queen of Farrehed. The man's audacity made him furious.

He was about to say something when he felt the soft hand of his wife on his arm.

'Oh, we have,' Eloise assured him. 'In fact, wasn't it Prince Imin who threw up on the sixteenth-century hand-woven tapestry at our engagement party, darling?' she asked of Odir.

'I had thought that was a cousin of the Duke of Cambridge, but now you mention it…' he replied with the affected haughty disdain she had once mocked him for.

'I believe it cost nearly two thousand pounds to get it cleaned,' she continued.

'It was more in the region of four, if I remember rightly.' Odir frowned, as if giving it deep thought.

'Two thousand pounds is *nothing* compared to what your father and brother cost Kalaran,' Imin spat angrily.

'You will address my husband by his proper title, Prince Imin,' Eloise commanded, and the ice in her voice was enough to cover the desert in frost.

Shockingly, a look of contrition passed over the man's features.

'Prince Imin, whatever deals my father made with yours I will take up directly with him,' Odir said.

'Oh, good. I had been concerned by recent news of his ill health. I do *so* hope that everything is okay, *Sheikh* Odir.'

Odir balled his hands into fists, only Eloise's grip on his arm anchoring him to the moment.

'Prince Imin, whilst it has been…*interesting* to see you again, I'm afraid there is someone over there with whom we have *important* things to discuss.'

With that snub, expertly delivered, Odir allowed himself to be led away by his wife.

This was what he had wanted from their union. A partnership—someone to stand beside him as he navigated the furious waters of the treacherous political sea wrought by his father's grief-stricken madness. That was what he had once seen in Eloise, and the glimpse of what might have been struck him dumb for just a moment.

And, then, he could scarcely believe that Eloise was giggling.

'Did you see the look on his face? I thought… I thought he was going to explode,' she said awkwardly in between bursts of laughter.

Odir felt an answering smile tugging at his lips. 'Would that he had…'

The mirth left her eyes, and something sober passed across her features.

'Is that what you've been dealing with?'

'What?' he asked, pulling himself from thoughts of his wife.

Was this not what he'd wanted to avoid? The all-consuming thread that wound around them until all he could see was her?

'When did things become so bad between Farrehed and Kalaran?' Eloise asked, wide eyed.

'After Jarhan's broken engagement and the recent trade agreements with Terhern things have been difficult,' Odir admitted.

It wasn't as if he were *confiding* in her—just that he was sharing things she would have to know once she returned to his side, he told himself.

'I hadn't realised…'

Odir let an exhausted breath escape. 'Do you *really* care, Eloise?'

Hurt slashed across her features. 'Of course I do, Odir. Farrehed became my country—they are my people too,' she said.

And in that moment Eloise realised the truth of her words. The time she had spent working with the desert tribes had shown her the strength of Farrehed's nomadic people.

Memories played with her, dancing across her skin the way the desert heat and sun once had, making her feel warm for the first time in what felt like years. Instead of burning and swelling up within the arid atmosphere, as she had once feared, Eloise had felt herself come alive. It had been a different sort of life from the one she had carved for herself in Zurich, but one she was surprised to find that she'd missed.

As they moved through the crowd Eloise slipped a practised smile onto her lips and scanned the people about her without really seeing anyone.

Until her eyes rested on a familiar face beside the bar and several threads of emotion wrapped themselves around her, pulling on her heart. Pleasure, sadness, surprise and a little fear. Jarhan was propping up the bar, a drink in his hand. She'd never seen Jarhan drink until that night six months ago. She wondered why he was here. It was strange that the two Farrehed Princes would be at such a minor event in the royal social calendar.

Jarhan met her eyes, expressing a wealth of emotion he'd never been able to give speech to. And just like that something eased around her heart. She could tell that he regretted that night more than anything. He could never have guessed at its shocking consequences, and Eloise felt sadness and pity rise within her.

A conciliatory smile threatened to lift the corners of her mouth. He had been such a source of comfort to her during her husband's long absences. He had been sweet, and funny, but always seemingly on the outskirts of the royal family. Never quite fitting in.

She supposed that it was quite possible he never would now. Not after the broken engagement that had followed the events of the night that had started all this…*mess*.

She felt Odir's heavy gaze on her and turned to him.

'Don't test me, *habibti*,' he whispered, with more anger than she had expected, or had ever heard in his voice before. 'I need your answer and I need it *now*.'

She looked back to Jarhan, saw in him the cost of duty and sacrifice, saw the weight of it almost crushing her friend, and knew then and there that she would not—could not—live like that.

'No, Odir. My answer is and always will be no. There's too much hurt—'

'Don't talk to me of hurt. Not tonight, Eloise.' He gave her a grim smile. 'I'm sorry, but you have left me with no choice.'

With that he departed, pushing his way through the throng of international dignitaries, socialites, actors and actresses—the world's wealthiest people, all waiting for *him*.

Without needing to request silence, he ensured the crowd was hushed and ready for his welcoming words.

Eloise was suddenly unsure. What had he meant by that?

At first her concern was so great she could not quite make out the words of his speech. She turned to Jarhan, but he was no longer by the bar and she couldn't see him anywhere. There was no comfort, no support—nothing and no one she could lean on. She was alone in a sea of people, and only the sound of her husband's voice tied her to the land.

Swells of gentle laughter crashed against her as the crowd lapped up the speech asking for generous donations to the charity Odir had spoken of earlier in the evening. The part of her mind engaged in the present dimly recognised that the initiative Odir was presenting had been a project she had started months before she had left. A project that *he* had seen to fruition.

Anger warred with confusion at the threat he had left her with, and she couldn't quite shake the feeling that she had been backed into an invisible corner. Eloise knew—just *knew*—that Odir was about to do or say something that she would never be free from.

Slowly her addled mind began to make out more and more of the words her husband was saying in his powerful but enticing voice.

'And it is because of you that healthcare in the

outer reaches of Farrehed will be able to continue. My country, my people and my family give thanks every day that you are willing to do business with my country, and for how important those relationships are not only for the present but also for the future. For the future generations of my people and my family.'

He paused, and found Eloise within the crowd.

Why was he talking so much about his family? she wondered. Why had his tone grown so soft, almost conspiratorial?

'A family,' he continued, 'that I am pleased to say will be increasing in number very soon.'

He held out an arm, gesturing towards her, and Eloise suddenly felt the weight of a thousand eyes, heavily and happily on *her*. The crowd erupted into a thunderous burst of applause. Words of congratulation and good wishes littered the air that had burst to life in the last few seconds.

And for the first time in her life Eloise forgot her practised smile, forgot how to play the game.

Because her husband had just told the world that she was pregnant.

CHAPTER FOUR

August 1st, 23.00-00.00, Heron Tower

IT WAS ALL Eloise could do not to burst into hysterical laughter. In fact there were tears pressing against the back of her eyes—she could feel them—and she thought…hoped…they were from laughter rather than anything deeper.

Noticing curiosity begin to enter the faces of the people surrounding her, she slipped a smile over the shock she felt and turned to thank them for their good wishes.

Eloise prayed that they would take the flush of anger painting her cheeks as one of happiness. She was going to kill him. Literally. The moment he came within two feet of her—which, she judged, was just about all the space she would need to ensure that he would *never* be able to have children and not just imaginary ones.

She would do considerable damage to his Crown Jewels. And not the ones he wore on his head.

She turned her gaze back to the podium, where

Odir had been standing only moments before, to see him slowly making his way through the crowds of people reaching out to slap him on the back, to shake his hand, congratulating him and his Princess on their good fortune.

Good fortune?

'Get out!'

The words he'd once said to her in anger, after incorrectly assuming she'd had an affair with his brother, now proved her salvation. She caught one glance from him and turned and fled—just as she had all those months before.

Knowing that there was no way he could get to her quickly without causing a scene, she stepped into the quiet corridor. Greeted with a silence that was more deafening than the noise the guests had created, she paused, not knowing where to go. One of Odir's guards appeared at the end of the hallway and she felt another one behind her.

Eloise took one step forward and then two back. She felt utterly trapped. She had been on the brink of freedom. She had been on the brink of getting everything she had ever wanted. And now it had been cruelly ripped away by her husband with just one sentence.

Looking ahead of her at Malik, she knew she would not be able to find help from that quarter. Not this time. Odir had claimed his bride without even having a wedding night.

And wasn't *that* the greatest irony of all? That he had declared his virgin bride pregnant with his child?

She saw a sliding door to the balcony that wrapped its way around the tall building and walked through it, instantly buffeted by a stiff breeze that cut through the confusion of the last few minutes and drenched her in night air.

Carefully designed heaters were placed near low-slung beige cotton-covered seats and sofas. Discreetly hidden canopies had been pulled back, out of the way of the strong wind that failed to take the heat out of the air. She walked to the furthest end of the balcony, gripping the metal railing, allowing the bite of cool metal to penetrate the numbness surrounding her.

And there, out in the dark alone, with London lit up before her—as if it too was celebrating the royal child she was supposed to be carrying—she felt every brush of the warm wind, pulling her hair loose from the pins she had bound it with, catching at the fabric of her dress, tugging it this way and that. She wished she could disappear—be swept across the far reaches of England and away from here.

For the love of God, she was a *virgin*—so very much the last person who was ready to become a mother, let alone to a child born from an immaculate conception!

It had taken the three weeks after their wedding night for Eloise to realise that her husband wouldn't come to her bed. Had her unpractised kiss horrified him that much? Had that been what drove him from her? Or had it all been lies? His promises of more than an arranged marriage designed solely to get his ring on her finger?

Eloise shook her head, as if to rid herself of the thoughts that had consumed her throughout the two lonely months she had spent in her marriage. Week after week, as one month had led to another, all she'd had were doubts and fears to keep her company. And they'd eaten away at her. A rejection so familiar.

She was so tired of feeling alone.

Even if in her deepest, darkest dreams she had ever considered returning to his side, there was no way she could inflict the kind of marriage they had on a child. Not after her own childhood. A child was someone to be protected—not someone to be manipulated or used as a political pawn.

But for just a second the image of a child with her fair skin and Odir's deep dark eyes flashed in her mind and took hold of her heart.

Furious at the thought of his wife evading him the moment he made his announcement, Odir extracted himself from the financially generous crowd.

Where *was* she? Why was his heart in his mouth and his pulse racing with something that might have been described as fear, had he been any other man?

Had he any other blood than Farrehed warrior ancestry coursing through his veins?

He caught Malik's eye. He pointed in the direction of the balcony.

The moment his eyes rested on Eloise's slim shoulders, flashing through the night like a beacon, he felt his pulse finally slow and he took his first breath. He drank in the sight of her, hair and skirts swirling around her thin frame.

When he had first caught sight of her in the stables, two years before, he had thought her slender. He had thought her beautiful. When his father had unknowingly re-introduced her to him later that day he'd been surprised. His father thought this slip of a girl could be his *wife*? He'd doubted at the time that she'd last even a month in the Farrehed heat.

Perhaps, had he paid attention to her surprising survival skills back then, he might have been better prepared for his wife.

Though looking at her now, he thought Eloise seemed lost. There was no other way to describe it. And just like that his conscience poked and prodded. There was a part of him that cursed the past—cursed all the steps that had brought them here. That had made him form those words around a ridiculous lie that would bind Eloise to him in a way her acceptance of his offer would not.

Malik appeared at his side.

'Are you sure this is what you want?' his old

friend asked again. As if he too realised the precipice they stood on.

No. Everything in him wanted to reject the path
he had set in motion just five minutes earlier. But he
didn't have a choice. He only had nine hours until the
press conference, and if she wasn't by his side when
it happened then fate would not be kind. He'd needed
to force the issue and he'd done just that.

'See to it that we are not disturbed.'

Malik bowed, and retreated behind the glass door.

Odir stepped towards her, momentarily blocked
by the wind as if even the elements were working
in her favour, trying to keep him from reaching her,
touching her. But that desire, that need, was a weakness he couldn't afford—had never been able to afford.

So he said words that he knew would keep her at
bay. 'Hardly the dutiful wife—running off just after
my speech, *habibti.*'

Eloise whirled round, hair flying, skirts billowing
in the wind. Odir hadn't realised how close he had
come to her and he should have. Because she shoved
at him with both her hands and only the surprise of
it allowed her enough force to push him back.

He felt Malik move behind him. Did he really
think that his slip of a wife was enough of a threat
to justify her removal? He raised his arm to ward
Malik off, even as almost laughably light blows
rained down on his chest.

'In all the time I have known you I have *never* known you to lie,' she hurled at him.

'No, that was *your* department.'

'Well, the world will be bitterly disappointed when instead of news of the next heir for Farrehed they'll be receiving news of the Prince's *divorce*.'

Eloise gave no heed to the fact that she was shouting. And that was something she never did.

'Never raise your voice, never cause a scene.'

Her father's directives were lost on her now, in the sheer fury of what had been done to her in the last ten hours.

She saw Malik shift on his feet behind Odir and it brought her back to the present immediately. Instantly she stepped away from her husband.

'Leave us, Malik,' her husband ordered with a familiar ruthlessness.

'But My—'

'Stop right there, Malik. I've told you. Leave.'

'It doesn't change a thing, you know. What you just said,' Eloise claimed desperately. 'I'll still leave.'

'I think you underestimate the sheer power of social media. Right now there are over a hundred of society's best-placed individuals drinking to our health and that of our unborn child. The news will spread quickly, and before the sun rises over the palace walls in Farrehed there will be a celebration the like of which has never been seen by my countrymen.'

With each word he stepped closer and closer to her, pushing her back further towards the rail of the balcony, building a wall around her from which she couldn't escape.

'And what happens when I fail to produce this immaculately conceived child? What happens in a few months' time when I'm not showing any signs of pregnancy? Are you going to tell another lie to cover it up? Will you expect me and your whole country to mourn the death of a lie?'

The horror of it was all too much for Eloise.

'You're an utter bastard, Odir.'

And that, it seemed, was what it took to push her husband over the edge.

'You think I *wanted* this?'

Now it was he who was shouting—and she had *never* heard her husband shout. Not even that fateful night when he'd ordered her from his sight and his palace.

'Do you think that I *enjoyed* telling that lie?'

'It doesn't really matter to me whether or not you got some perverse enjoyment out of it. I will not agree to this. It's the twenty-first century, Odir. You can't expect to lie, bribe and cheat me back to your side.'

'You really think that after this you'd be able to leave and live some kind of normal life? Go back to whatever man you have holed up in Switzerland?'

'What man? *Seriously?* You think I've been living with someone in Zurich? Tell me, Odir, is there anyone that I *haven't* slept with other than yourself?'

He glared at her in the light of the moon.

'And when this immaculately conceived child *does* make an appearance will you be asking for a DNA test?'

His response cut through her like a knife.

'You will, of course, undergo medical assessment before any child of mine is conceived.'

The horror, the invasion of her privacy that he so carelessly described was sickening. So much so that she couldn't help the bitter laugh that dropped from her lips.

'And just how, exactly, were you planning on having this child with a woman you can barely look at, let alone touch?'

But even as the words left her lips the memory of his lips against hers earlier that evening sprang to life. Eloise relived every second of it—the way his tongue had stroked against hers, the way he had brought to life a passion she'd only imagined she was capable of. And she hated herself for that. How she hated the way her lips had clung to him as if she were dying of thirst and only he could quench it.

'Were you hoping that you could do this, too, without being present? Will you call in the doctors to help you with the problem? You couldn't even give me a wedding night!'

'I didn't have a choice! What would you have had

me do? Turn my back on my country? Let it descend into war with Terhren?'

He bit back a curse that felt heavy on his tongue. For that was so close—*too* close—to the truth of what had nearly happened that night.

'No, but you could have *said* something. You could have explained.'

'There was no time. I couldn't have returned to you even if I'd wanted to.'

But that wasn't the truth was it? his mind whispered accusingly. He could have gone to her. Explained. But he'd been overcome by their shared passion. He'd nearly taken her there in the hallway, where anyone might have seen.

The desire between them had always been powerful. It had been there at their first meeting in the stables. It had been there during those stolen moments he'd found with her during their engagement. Pulsing between them.

And it had been there when his aide had come to find him the night of their wedding. The aide who had interrupted that kiss…the kiss he'd never been able to forget. Even the news that his father had invaded Terhren had only just been enough to douse the need he'd had for Eloise that night.

The need that spoke volumes as to how quickly and how much she had come to mean to him in such a short space of time. A need that he'd promised himself he would never succumb to. Not after he had seen the consequences of such need through the grief-stricken madness that had descended over his father when he'd lost his wife. When he and Jarhan had lost their mother.

'Okay, Odir,' she said, in mock appeasement. 'Fine—you didn't have time to tell me what was going on. You didn't have time to ask an aide to send me word as I sat there that night, waiting for you to come back, in a dress I couldn't undo by myself. I had to cut it off with *scissors*, Odir! But I'll give you that night. What of the next? And the next? And the one after that?'

'It took three weeks, Eloise—*three weeks* to talk the Sheikh of Terhren down from a war that would have ruined both our countries.'

'And which war were you preventing *after* those three weeks? What was it that stopped you from explaining to me what was going on then? From telling me what you were dealing with? You lied to me, Odir. Before our marriage you told me it would be a partnership. You told me we would share the royal burden together.'

And he had meant it. He had meant his promise to her then. But he had underestimated just how far his father's destruction had spread. Abbas had used Odir's preoccupation with Eloise, with the wedding, with building the kind of relationship he wanted— the one she now taunted him with—against him, and had laid plans that Odir had spent the last six months ruthlessly undoing.

His conscience poked at him again. She was right.

He should have informed her of the extent to which Farrehed had been in trouble. He could have even taken her with him on diplomatic missions. Had he been able to trust himself—had he been able to control the desire that whipped up a storm between them every time she came near...

At the heart of it, Odir was genuinely afraid that if he'd allowed himself to dive into the desire that burned between them he would have become his father.

But he couldn't admit that to his wife now. He couldn't afford to show such weakness. Not at a time when she, unknowingly, held so much power.

'I couldn't have returned to you even if I'd wanted to.'

She hated how those words had made her feel. Hated it that he still had the power to hurt her with callously delivered words.

'I did what I had to, Eloise. As I am doing now.'

'And I am doing what *I* have to. There is no way I would bring a child into this...*marriage*. You clearly think so little of me you still believe I am a woman who slept with your own brother—'

His arm came up between them and slashed through the night air.

'Don't speak of it. The past is the past. It's dead to me. It doesn't matter. All that matters now is tomorrow and that you are by my side for it.'

'I won't let you shut me up—not this time. Nothing happened between me and Jarhan. *Nothing*.'

For the first time Odir acknowledged that something wasn't quite ringing true. If she really wanted a divorce from him she'd admit to having an affair with Jarhan, wouldn't she? But she was defending herself against the accusation—defending herself in a way that he'd never given her the chance to do that night. Was it possible that he'd been wrong? That he'd misinterpreted the situation?

'You once said that we could be more than our fathers—that we didn't have to follow the manipulative paths they once had. But *you*, of them all, are the worst. Because *they* didn't lie about their intentions. So, no,' she said, shaking her head. 'No, I *won't* return to your side. So you've told the world, Odir, that I am pregnant with your child? I don't care. I don't care what they say about me.'

And she realised that was the truth. She hadn't lied to him when she'd told him she'd changed. She had found herself in Zurich and that had endowed her with a sense of self and a strength that even the Prince of Farrehed couldn't take away.

'You can take your lies, your money, and stick it up your…your royally wiped arse.'

'My *royally wiped*…? Are you kidding me right now?'

'No, Odir. I'm serious. *Very* serious. I *will* have that divorce. No matter what you do or say.'

Out across the river Big Ben began its peal, chiming the twelve strikes of midnight. Each tone crashed through him like an embodiment of impending doom.

Bong.

'No, *habibti*. You won't. Because you can't.'

Bong.

Each chime prevented him from taking a breath. Each chime punctuated the air between them just as her words had.

'Why do you need this so badly, Odir? Why can't you let me go?'

She was always going to ask him the question, and he was always going to have to answer it.

There was an innocence, a wealth of curiosity in her words, because she knew nothing of what she was asking. But he would answer her. Just as he would answer the questions of the rabid press in eight hours' time.

'Because, Eloise, at seven this morning, Swiss time, my father died. I am now King of Farrehed.'

CHAPTER FIVE

August 2nd, 00.00-01.00, Heron Tower

FOR THE SECOND time in as many hours Eloise felt as if the world had turned on its axis and everything she'd thought she knew, thought she could trust in, was gone.

'Dead? How can that be?' she asked.

Despite her feelings for him, it seemed utterly impossible to her that Abbas, King of Farrehed, was gone. He had been so full of grit and determination. Even if that determination had often pointed in the wrong direction.

Odir's father had seemed like an indestructible force of nature—not one who would ever leave this world. She knew that Odir and his father had had a difficult relationship. One that had been fraught with undercurrents she had barely been privy to. Odir had never discussed his father with her. Not once. Even before their marriage.

'Three weeks ago he suffered a stroke and fell into

a coma. The doctors tried everything they could,'
Odir said, blocking the painful memories of the last
time he had spoken with his father and instead focusing on the words the doctor had shared with him
over the phone only eighteen hours before.

He looked at his wife and suddenly wanted to
reach out to her. Offer comfort at her obvious distress. And then he realised how ridiculous that was.
Because surely it was *he* who should need comfort?
He who should be in distress? But he searched his
soul and all he felt was numb. A numbness that had
descended long before his argument with his father
three weeks before.

'Why have we not heard about this? What are
you doing in England? You should be in Farrehed.'

Her voice peppered him with the questions and
accusations he had aimed at himself over and over
again that day. But discussions with his brother, with
his closest advisors, had all reached the same conclu-
sion. For him to return to Farrehed and assume the
throne—without contention from the tribes on the
outskirts of Farrehed, from the neighbouring countries who were still trying to cash in on the secret
deals his father had done—he would very much need
Eloise by his side. To present a traditional, perfect
royal family picture.

After all these years and everything he had done
to prove himself—everything he had done in the
name of bettering his country—it was still absolutely

nothing, almost insignificant, without this woman on his arm.

'I will return to Farrehed later today. With my Queen beside me.'

And finally he could see, dawning on his wife's beautiful face, the true implications of this news. The *true* need he had for her to be by his side.

Even with shock after shock raining down on her, it surprised Eloise to find out just how much that hurt. That it wasn't because of her, and it wasn't born of any feelings for her that he wanted her back.

Even though she had suspected some ulterior need beneath Odir's proposal, it had never been this. And it was then that Eloise realised she had been cherishing a small hope that perhaps her husband had wanted her for more than just a means to an end.

Not that she should be focusing on that. Odir had lost his father—Farrehed had lost its King. Eloise realised just as much as her husband clearly did that there was no way the country would survive without its Queen.

Even if she *was* only a means to an end Eloise wasn't sure that she could turn her back on the country where she had spent two years. When she'd worked for the medical foundation she had found something that had made sense to her. She had fallen in love with the people and had loved Farrehed as much as she did her birth country.

But was that enough? Could she really sacrifice her happiness for Farrehed?

Eloise wanted to sink down onto one of the small white squares that littered the balcony, feeling the weight of just half of what Odir must be feeling, but she didn't. She couldn't. She had been brought up better than that. She couldn't crumble. Not if Odir had not.

'Obviously you need some time to process this, Eloise,' Odir said.

'What? More time than you have allowed yourself?'

'Stop fighting me. Please.'

It was the first time she'd ever heard that word fall from his lips. *Please.* There was something so resigned about the way he said it. So…so mournful, she realised.

Odir watched his wife's shoulders begin to shake, as if tiny tremors were working their way through her body. He couldn't tell whether it was from the cold or the shock. Though even *he* recognised the unseasonable English heat—if it could be called heat—that surrounded them in the midnight air.

He slipped off his jacket and placed it over her slight frame, pulling it tight around her. Whether it was this simple act of caring for his wife, or the proximity of her to his body, he couldn't tell, but he felt an unwelcome curl of desire unfurl just beneath his skin. It started in his hands, where they had come to rest just beneath her breasts, and spread out like a fire lighting his skin and his lungs in the same moment.

But it wasn't just desire. It was something much darker and more dangerous than that. It was anticipation. And Odir found himself wondering, not for the first time, what it would be like to lose himself completely in his wife's body. What it would be like to plunge his tongue into deeper depths than his wife's soft mouth. What it would be like to feel Eloise shiver beneath his touch with something other than cold.

Odir met his wife's eyes and saw the compassion and the sympathy held there and he hated it. Hated it that his wife was looking at him in the one way that could undo him. Damn her—why wasn't she feeling it too? The same madness that was so tempting to him…more tempting than anything he had felt since his wedding night.

And then, as if his thought had been spoken out loud, he saw the moment that she felt it too. Her eyes widened—just a fraction. Had they been in a crowded room he doubted very much that anyone else would have noticed, would have seen the subtle change that came over her features and sent a spark of satisfaction rampaging through his body. Here was something secret—just between his wife and him.

Her eyes, usually a bright shade of blue, grew

dark, almost matching the night sky behind her. Her pupils widened and he saw the flicker of her pulse quicken beneath the soft indentation in her jaw. For a fanciful moment he believed that their hearts were beating in time, and cursed himself for the thought.

'We need to leave,' he said, shutting down the madness that—had he had more to drink—he would have blamed on alcohol.

He removed his hands away from where they rested and walked towards the glass door that separated them from the party within. Malik and one of the other guards were stationed either side of the door, and as they passed through Odir registered the soft tones of the party still in full swing with surprise. It seemed almost inconceivable that the world was continuing to turn despite the events of the last few hours.

Turning away from the muffled noise, he stalked towards the lift, and once again Eloise stepped in beside him. In the mirror, she looked dishevelled. As if it had been he rather than the wind who had run his hands through her hair, who had pushed aside her skirts.

He clenched his fists and ordered himself back under control as the lift arrived at its destination.

In the hallway another guard held the door to his suite open, and once again Odir marched straight into the darkened rooms and, control be damned, headed straight for the whisky.

He listened for the sounds of Eloise behind him

and realised that she was the first person that he'd told about his father's death.

Jarhan had been with him when the doctor had conveyed the news that had set his every action today in motion. Odir had been able to tell, when he'd seen his aide, that he had already been informed by the medical staff—in the event that the Princes would need further support. And now, between his aide and his bodyguards, who had been sworn to secrecy, it left the number of people who knew about his father's death at a total of twelve—including the doctor and nurse.

It felt so strange. The man he'd spent years hating, the man who had almost obliterated any happy childhood memories—memories of when his father had *not* been the monster he had become the day his wife tragically died—was now gone from this world. He wondered, not for the first time, if it would have been easier had he not had those happy memories. If Abbas's later actions had truly killed any knowledge of the man he had once been. The father he had once been.

'It's okay to mourn him, Odir.'

A bitter laugh erupted, unbidden, from his lips, searing his flesh with its intensity.

'Thank you for your permission, but I mourned the loss of my father years ago—the moment he stopped being a father and a husband and became a widowed king.'

He crossed the room in two strides and went to

the drinks cabinet, with a determination to wash the taste of grief and anger from his palate with whisky. Unthinking, he put ice into two crystal-cut glasses, poured a generous amount of amber liquid into both, and passed one to Eloise. The weight of the glass was oddly satisfying, and he was left oddly bereft when she took it from him.

He looked up and found Eloise watching him through narrowed eyes.

'You think that a cruel thing to say? You think *me* cruel?' he asked.

He was genuinely curious. For although once he might have claimed to know her thoughts, with the changes the last six months had brought to her he honestly couldn't tell.

'No. On the contrary,' Eloise said, so quietly he had to strain to hear her. 'I think it an eminently practical thing to mourn the loss of a person who has changed irrevocably.'

Odir was surprised. He'd thought that she would try to comfort him with gentle words and reassuring sympathy, which would have been utterly false to his own feelings, and he was thankful she hadn't. Thankful that she hadn't tried to contradict him. Thankful that she hadn't tried to reassure him that *'grief was a natural part of life'*.

His mind replayed the words of his father's nurse as she had tried to offer some comfort to her new Sheikh. Perhaps, he realised with a silent laugh, she had been vying for a position within the royal household and he had been too numb to realise it.

'What was he like?'

Her words drew him back.

'The father you mourned, not the King you lost.'

Part of him didn't want to go there. Didn't want to revisit memories he would find painful. But, even though his heart avoided it, he scanned his memory for a time when his father *hadn't* been so stricken with grief that it had rotted every good thing about him. And there, just as it had always been, was a memory waiting to be found. It led him to the next memory, and the next, as if a string of lights were being turned on, one after the other.

'He laughed,' Odir said, sounding almost as surprised as he felt. 'It was the sound of his laugh—I'll never forget it. It was deep. Deep and joyful. Perhaps not two words that you would associate with the man you met. And he smiled. It was never going to be a perfect smile. As a child he'd been kicked by a horse—a vicious kick that broke his jaw. Not that that stopped him from riding—or smiling. Though according to my mother it stopped him talking for a good while.'

Odir realised that he too was smiling until fresher, newer, memories overlaid the past.

'It's that memory that is the hardest. Because had I not known a father who smiled, who laughed and played with his wife and children, then I wouldn't have known anything different. Instead I watched a powerful, kind, generous man disintegrate into a bitter, paranoid, destructive man who ruined everything he touched because he had lost his love.'

And that was why Odir had been happy with a marriage based on nothing so dangerous as emotions. Because his father had proved over and over again just how damaging love could be to a man—to a king. And whether or not he felt desire for this woman—the woman who had betrayed him in the most awful way—he was certainly sure of one thing. He would make sure that she could not incite in him anything near love. Even if there had been feelings that might have grown into something more, then they had been killed dead the day he'd found her with his brother.

Despite his silence, Eloise could trace the feelings crossing her handsome husband's features. And for a moment she was lost in his words, wondering if her own father had ever been like that. If perhaps that was why her mother had chosen to stay with him—desperate to see traces of another man, the one she had first fallen in love with.

For a strange moment, she felt impossibly close to her mother and couldn't explain why. But then darker memories returned—of her father and his manipulations, her mother's constant escape into prescription drugs to dull the edge of whatever emotion she wanted not to feel. Each time her hopes of being loved and wanted for who she was had been dashed, again and again.

She dragged her thoughts away from her own life and returned them to Odir's.

'I hadn't realised that things were so bad,' she said into the dark room.

Her words seemed to reach her husband a long moment later, and she realised that she had echoed the same sentiment she'd expressed upon their encounter with Prince Imin. Had she been so preoccupied with her own wants and needs that she had failed to grasp the true significance of her husband's absence?

'Jarhan and I have worked for years with the council to protect Farrehed from our father's paranoia and bad decision-making. Or even lack of decision-making. For some time he simply retreated and made decisions about the governing of Farrehed from his ivory tower.'

'Is that what you were doing in the first months of our marriage? Is that why you were so busy?'

'Had I not been so distracted by our engagement, our wedding, my father might not have been able to muster enough support to make an incursion on to Terhren soil. He might not have been able to undo the hard work Jarhan and I had put in to redeem Farrehed in the eyes of her allies.'

Eloise's mind flew to the spaces in between his words, the meaning she so desperately wanted to find.

Did he blame her? Did he blame their relationship—whatever form it had taken—for what Sheikh Abbas had been able to do?

'I was trying to hold the country together by a thread. A thread I had to weave without my father seeing me as a usurper.'

In his mind's eye, Odir watched his father hurl a priceless antique vase gifted to him by the Egyptian Ambassador across the room and watched the pieces shatter and scatter across the floor. It had been illustrative of his father's sheer fury at the thought of his eldest son trying to take his place.

In his madness he had called him all the names under the sun—things that he would never repeat to a living soul, not even his brother. And it had brought to life the awful, terrible truth. That, yes, Odir *had* wanted his father gone—he *had* wanted to usurp his father's position so that he could stop him damaging their beloved country. But not because he had wanted that power for himself—as his father had thought.

'I thought it was because you didn't want me.'

Eloise's voice broke through, the hurt her tone failed to conceal crashing against wounds already salted with grief.

'*Want* you? I *always* wanted you, Eloise.'

His words shocked her. Cut through the months of silence and absence. Cut through the fears that some-

how she had not been what he wanted. That in spite
of the attraction she'd thought they'd shared it was
a figment of her imagination.

'I wanted you so much that I nearly turned my
back on my country. Do you know how hard it was
for me to walk away that night? I nearly didn't!'

Shock marked her features, but he couldn't stop, the
words seemingly ripped from the past and falling
unrestrained from his lips.

'From the moment of my birth I was brought up
to protect this country. My father educated me in
leadership, and I was sent to university to gain an
understanding of politics and economics for the betterment of my country. Everything was about protecting the people of Farrehed, even when I had to
protect it against my own father. But I never thought
that I might have to protect it against *me*. Against
the desire I felt for you. In that moment just before
I left the palace for Terhren I would have let it burn
for just one more taste of you. Just like my father
would have done.'

His breath was unaccountably tight within his
chest.

'Every single thing I have done or not done has
been for Ferrehed. I can never become the selfish
man my father was. I will *never* be that man. And I
will never make the same mistakes he did.'

'And if you weren't?'

'If I weren't what?'

'A ruler. If you weren't bound by rules and duty and convention what would you be? What would you want?'

You. The word came unbidden to his mind. Even before their marriage—even before she had been presented to him as the perfect wife—he had been intrigued by the pale, silky-skinned woman before him.

He saw her as she had been then, standing in the summer sun in the dusty stable yard, taunting him with her words, teasing him with her smiles. She had brought brightness back to the palace that had been like a dark kingdom, holding its breath under the weight of a year's long grief. If he were honest with himself he knew he had held her at a distance because she had truly been the only threat to the barriers around his heart.

It was as if his thoughts had reached out into the air around them and changed something. Something that had passed between them. He could see now that Eloise understood why he needed this marriage. All bribery and pretence was done. She had accepted that, he could tell.

But beyond that he could see his own desire reflected in her eyes, and the temptation to sink into it, to give in and stop fighting, was so great. How bad would it be if just for once he could simply take what he wanted and damn the consequences?

His mind flew back to earlier in the evening, when he had greeted her with a kiss that had been intended to humiliate, to punish, but had done nothing of the sort. The kick of adrenaline—purer than any daredevil ride, any hit of alcohol—had flooded his system, blocking all thoughts completely.

And for once Odir was desperate to feel something other than all the swirling emotions brought about by his father's death, this conversation, all his doubts about his wife. He wanted to feel something else. Her skin beneath his hands...her lips beneath his...her body beneath his body. Perhaps if he gave in—if he allowed himself to have her, even just once—it would resolve his need. Perhaps he would finally be free of the chains his desire for her had wound around him.

And for the first time since he had placed that ring on his wife's finger he couldn't think of a reason not to.

He closed the distance between them in two powerful strides, and before his beautiful, treacherous wife could do anything to stop him he slid his hand into the hair at the base of her neck, glided his palm against her cheek, pulled her lips close to his and sank into a heaven he had no business entering.

CHAPTER SIX

August 2nd, 01.00-02.00, Heron Tower

FOR A MOMENT—just a moment—Eloise was completely taken aback. This was nothing like the kiss he had punished her with when he had first seen her downstairs at the party. Nor the kiss from their wedding night.

She wondered whether she had somehow conjured it from her deepest fantasies. For in a sense it was the way she had always wanted him to kiss her. There was a rawness, an urgency about it that called to something deep within her. She could feel the recklessness in his touch—could feel it in the depths of her mouth, plundered by his tongue with an onslaught so sensual, so incredible, that it simply could not be real.

His hands shifted, the palm at her neck slipping down to the centre of her back, bringing her body fully flush against his own. She felt the hard planes of his stomach against her soft skin, the press of his arousal, and it wasn't enough.

She wanted more.

And for that she hated him.

She felt fury race through the blood in her veins. Anger that he had withheld this from her. That he had denied them this. Denied them something that could have cut through all the deceit, all the lies, all the unspoken truths that had come between them. He had denied them something that would have brought them together in the way that men and women had been brought together for all the centuries of the world's existence.

Eloise was furious—furious at all the things that life had placed just out of her reach, the things that she'd never been able to have or to indulge in. His tongue wrapped around her own, filling her in a way that promised a different kind of fulfilment, and in that moment of fear—fear that he wouldn't seek complete fulfilment—her hands came to life, clutching at the shirt he wore, pulling him to her just as powerfully as he was pulling her to him.

She felt Odir take in a ragged breath without breaking the seal of their kiss, knowing that the air they shared came together in a way more intimate than they had ever been with each other.

She opened her eyes and saw him lost to the kiss, just as she had been. His dark skin betrayed him with a faint flush, his closed eyes, framed by impossibly dark eyelashes, were hiding the secrets hidden there.

It was all too much. She wanted to see him—

wanted to know that he was driven by this uncon-
strained passion as much as she was.

She pushed Odir back, breaking their contact and
forcing him to look at her. Their breathing, ragged
and uncontrolled, the only sound in the darkened
room. And she got what she asked for. In his gaze
she could see anger, accusation and fury, all rimmed
with need and a fire that finally she knew would not
be so easily put out.

Their masks were off. All the hurt, the pain, all
the passion held at bay for so long—too long—was
laid bare between them. Suddenly the anger swelled
to life within her and she lifted her palms to his chest
and pushed. Pushed and punched, again and again,
and he just stood there, taking each blow, each strike.

'Are you done?' he demanded into the darkened
room.

'No. I've not even begun,' she promised him.

'Good.'

He gathered her wrists in his strong hands and
drew her back to him. Crushed her mouth with his
and began his reckless, sensual onslaught once again.
His hands came around her slim waist and he pulled
her from her feet up against his body, blocking all
thought of what might have been had it not been for
their fathers, had not been for all the lies.

It was just them in the suite—no audience, no
press, no witnesses—and Eloise finally demanded the
pleasure that she'd waited for, longed for all this time.

Even as his fingers roamed over the black silk fabric of her dress, separating his skin from hers by the smallest distance possible, her mind raced. This was her husband—a man who thought the very worst of her, of whom she had thought the very worst... Perhaps they could take this one moment, this chance to indulge in the deepest fantasies which had kept her awake night after night in the palace as she had lain alone.

Perhaps tonight she could forget that she was a virgin, that she was innocent—forget that the whole of her body was trembling in a heady mixture of anticipation and fear. She knew he did not think her innocent. And for the most shocking moment she wanted to have had that experience—wanted to be a woman who knew what she was doing.

Eloise was so tired of being scared, of being helpless. Perhaps if she faked knowledge, faked the sophistication he believed her to have, then she could just let go...

Odir felt as if he were letting go of something that he couldn't—wouldn't—put a name to. He felt as if all his desire, all his need, was pouring out of him and being eaten, consumed whole, by the woman in his hands. And still it wasn't enough—this kiss wasn't enough.

He had been able to take the soft punches her hands had thrown at his chest. He had been able to take her anger because it matched his own. But he hadn't been able to take that look in her eyes when she'd watched him. So he had stopped her with another kiss.

He stepped back, without breaking the hold his lips had on hers, and ran his hands down the front of her chest, over her beautiful breasts—just enough of a handful to rest in his palms, as if they were made for him and him alone. Her nipples pebbled beneath his touch and he cursed, because touching was no longer enough.

He followed the path his hands had taken with open-mouthed kisses, his tongue meeting silk and skin where the two pieces of material covered her breasts. He pushed one of the sections aside with his thumb and lapped at her soft skin—purer than silk, purer than *any* silk he had ever touched—and revelled in the power he had as he heard her soft gasp echo in the room.

He had never been so hard in his life. He should have known that this woman of all women could do that to him. But all thoughts flew from his head when she arched her back, whether consciously or not, pressing her breast closer and deeper against him.

He couldn't hold back any more.

He yanked the material aside and took her hard nipple into his mouth, drawing on it as if he were a drowning man. Again she groaned, louder this time and more urgent, as if her body was calling to his… as if she did not know what she was calling for.

In the shadows of the room her pale skin gleamed like the purest white marble and he wanted to see more of it. He could see a soft shaft of light from the bedroom through the darkness, but he knew right then that he wouldn't be able to make it that far.

Taking her mouth once again with his, he pushed her back, making her legs step in time with his until he felt her stop, pressed against the dark mahogany table framed by the floor-to-ceiling glass vista behind it. He lifted her up and sat her on the table, pushing apart her legs with his strong thighs. Not that he needed to. Her legs were already willingly spread, granting him access to her.

In the dark room he watched her hands come up to his white shirt, and with satisfaction he saw that her fingers were trembling—just as he had wanted them to be earlier that evening, not from cold but from the same insane desire that gripped him.

Impatient to feel her skin against his own, he reached up and ripped the shirt apart, sending small buttons flying across the room. A look passed over Eloise's face and he wondered momentarily if it was fear. But that couldn't be right, and with a split second's decisiveness he changed tack.

He wanted her blind with desire. He wanted to hear her call his name before he entered her, before he found solace inside her. He wanted to know that it was he and only he who could drive her wild.

He reached behind her and swept everything from

the table. All of it. The lamp, the pens and paper from earlier, when he had been preparing the speech for his press conference. He wanted all of it gone.

He wanted to hear the cries of pleasure he knew were waiting on his wife's tongue. He wanted to block all thoughts—hers and his—of the future that was to come and simply immerse them both in this heady, impossible passion that threatened to consume them whole.

He pushed her back against the smooth wooden table top and gathered her small feet in his hands. Such delicate feet...he had never realised. He smoothed away the silk of her dress, pushing it up the shapely calves he found hidden beneath the material, up further past thighs of such smooth skin that it was almost enough to undo him right there and then.

Eloise moaned from the table, almost rising up to greet him, but he placed one palm on the plane of flat skin between her breasts, gently pushing her back down.

Hard. The thought came into his mind once more. He had never been so hard. So turned on. And for that he would ensure that she felt exactly the same. He relished the delicious punishment he was about to bestow upon his wife.

He pushed the skirts of her dress over her hips and found the tiny black thong covering the core of her femininity. And that was what he found there— nothing but utter femininity...

* * *

Eloise felt so incredibly open and exposed it almost took her breath away. She felt the heady combination of being both utterly vulnerable and incredibly powerful. Her husband—the most imposing, commanding man she knew—wanted to please her in this way, was looking at her with lust-filled eyes…eyes that promised and brooked no argument.

Somehow, in a room that was silent of everything other than the sounds of their harsh breathing and the desire-fuelled cries that seemed to come from somewhere other than her, even though she knew it *was* her, he was telling her what he was going to do. He was giving her time both to anticipate and prepare herself, for there was no stopping him now.

That was what his look told her before he dropped to his knees and began pressing open-mouthed kisses along thighs that had never even known the touch of a man, let alone the hot trail of his tongue.

His lips moved away from her thighs and she felt him press that same mouth that had toyed with her only moments before against her wet core. She felt the pressure of his tongue through thin fabric of her thong and she cursed it—shifting her hips beneath the gentle pressure he maintained, desperate for him to remove the last barrier between them. She cried out loud—a keening sound that she could not recognise as herself—and somehow she knew that he was smiling.

She shifted her legs, brought her foot up to rest against the corner of the table and used it to push herself further into his kiss.

And he took instant advantage, allowing the lift of her bottom to pull the tiny thong down around her thighs. Her fingers moved of their own volition, reaching for the thin ties to pull it off, but his hand reached out and held her, stopping her in her tracks.

'No,' he commanded.

With her thighs held in place by the binding of her underwear, stretched almost to the breaking point, he dropped his head and with one long stroke of his tongue almost brought her to orgasm. *Almost*—because she knew he could tell how close she was and he stopped.

He was playing with her, and in that moment she both loved him and hated him for it.

Never in all his life had he tasted anything so sweet. He knew how close she was to orgasm, and thanked his lucky stars that she had no idea how close *he* was. With his thumbs he massaged the inviting hollows just above the juncture of her thighs, opening her further to him. He let the pad of his thumb caress that delicate bundle of nerves and was surprised by the jolt that ran through her.

Never before had he felt so powerful. Never before had he seen such an instant reaction to his touch. And he couldn't help himself. Again he thrust out his tongue and swept it across her—this time not for her but very much for him. And he was rewarded with the one thing he had wanted since he had been mad enough to touch his lips to hers earlier that evening.

His name on her lips echoed out into the room and he swept his tongue across her once more, just to hear it again. He wasn't disappointed.

'Please,' she whispered, her voice fractured by her breathing. 'I want to feel you. I want to feel you inside me.'

She was begging now, and he'd never heard anything so good.

He smiled against her thigh, shaking his head. He couldn't speak—he didn't want anything to intrude against the sound of her pleas.

He plunged a finger into her and felt glorious as her hips thrust her further and deeper against him. Her thighs, still bound with the ties of her thong, began to shake and her chest lifted from the table.

He lifted his free hand and placed it back on her chest, sweeping beneath the material of the halter-neck and gently tightening his fingers around the taut nipple he found there...

With one last stroke of his tongue Odir pushed her over the edge of an abyss she hadn't realised she'd been on the brink of ever since he'd taken her mouth with his. She felt herself shatter into a thousand pieces, totally overridden by a million sensations that she couldn't put into words. She was mindless

with a pleasure she had never experienced before—
so much so that she didn't have time. Time to think…
time to prepare herself, to warn him.

He had slipped the thong from her thighs and cast
it aside. He had undone the fastening of his trousers,
and stepped out of them and his underwear. He had
freed himself and positioned himself between her
thighs. He had waited until her body was racked
again with the aftershock of her orgasm, and now
he entered her with one long thrust.

It was the sound of her cry, so different from any that
had come before it, that alerted him to the fact that
something was wrong. It was only then that he registered the thin barrier he had pushed his way past in
his eagerness to find his pleasure, to find his fulfilment. And it was only then that he stopped himself
completely. Holding himself impossibly still when
everything in him—*everything*—screamed for him
to continue.

'Eloise…?'

'I'm sorry. I'm so sorry. It'll pass. Just…just don't
move. Not yet.'

He cursed out loud, the words falling harshly into
the air about them. And then he cursed again.

He watched her head fall to the side, as if avoid-
ing him.

'Look at me,' he commanded. Because he needed
her to.

He needed to see it in her eyes. He needed confirmation of the suspicion that, if he was brutally honest with himself, had been creeping up on him since their second kiss.

'*Habibti*,' he said, softening his voice, smoothing over the harshness of his curses. 'Look at me, please…' He asked this time.

And when she looked at him he knew. He could see both the truth and the accusation in her gaze.

He made to withdraw, but her hand stopped him.

'Don't…please. Just…just a minute more,' she requested.

And in that moment he probably would have given her the world, had she asked.

The pain receded as quickly and as suddenly as it had come. She felt him so deeply within her, filling her, joining with her in a way she had never imagined. She felt connected to him in a way that words and promises could never have done.

She flexed her hips experimentally and felt him jerk within her. He cursed again, and she almost smiled. She had never once seen her powerful, proud husband lose control enough to curse in such a way, and within the space of seconds he had turned the very air blue.

She felt him move, reaching further and deeper than before, but so very differently. The movement held none of the recklessness from before—none of the unleashed fury that had risen between them. It was almost caring and honest. And it was all the things that she didn't want, because it would hurt so much more when this stopped and they were back to sniping at each other. She didn't think she would survive it—not now that she knew he was capable of this.

She pushed herself up from the desk, still luxuriating in the feel of him inside her. He backed up, giving her room, and lifted the dress over her head and arms and tossed it aside. He circled his arms around her. And finally—after all this time, all the things he had done to her—they were skin to skin, her breasts pressed against the rough hair covering his chest.

His hands lowered and came around her bottom, bringing her closer, impossibly closer, and he was now completely and fully within her. She wrapped her arms around his broad chest, and there in his arms she felt safer than she had ever felt in her entire life. No matter what happened next, no matter what happened later that day, and the day after, and the day after that, they would have this moment. Nothing would take that from her.

He started to rock his hips towards her and she felt the tendrils of another orgasm reach out within her. Her breath came out in harsh gasps, and the sound of a cry—his or hers, she could not tell—wrapped itself around them, weaving a sensuality between them that far exceeded her wildest fantasies.

Every time he moved he pressed against the sensitive nerves at her core, exciting her both within and without. Eloise felt that she was once again on a precipice—on the cusp of something that was just out of her reach. It mirrored the feeling she'd had earlier that night, of how everything she had ever wanted was just beyond her, and she wondered whether with this man she might just find it.

She knew then that it was nothing to do with sex. It wasn't completion, it wasn't orgasm, and just before she could finish the thought—just before she could feel the ache and the pain of realising that it was his heart she was looking for, the one thing that he would never let her have—he drove her over the edge, taking her with him as they both found orgasm at the same time.

CHAPTER SEVEN

August 2nd, 02.00-03.00, Heron Tower

ODIR'S MIND WAS completely blank. He'd just been rocked by the most intense orgasm of his entire life, and yet somewhere in his mind coherent thought was trying to break through. But he didn't want it to. He knew where those thoughts would take him and he wasn't yet ready for them.

The stirrings of guilt and unease were persistent, though, and he knew he needed space—needed time that he simply didn't have—to work through the revelations of the past few minutes.

His wife had been a virgin.

That was an inescapable fact. How had he got it so wrong? *Had* he got it wrong? Just because she'd been an innocent, it didn't mean that she hadn't somehow enticed his brother to behave so recklessly—hadn't bewitched Malik to break his solemn oath to Odir. And it certainly didn't explain why she had fled Farrehed for another country and effectively disappeared for six months.

But if he was wrong…if he had misjudged her…

He had coerced her into coming here, demanded without explanation, without consideration of any feeling on Eloise's part, that she resume her wifely duties, bear his heirs, just so he could be King, just so he could get what he needed to secure his country's future…

What did that make him? If he could so badly mistreat his wife, what would he do to his country?

The ground shifted beneath his feet and his stomach lurched. But it wasn't the ground. It was his wife. She was beginning to stir in his arms. Arms that were still circled around her slim frame as if his life depended on it.

He slowly disentangled himself from her—and he hated the small part of him that wanted to do more than just put physical distance between them. That was a coward's way out, and he was *not* a coward.

Eloise glanced up at her husband, the light from a pale moon revealing his features under its touch. Thoughts were crossing his mind—hundreds of them, showing little glimpses of how he felt. She could see doubt mar the skin over his high cheekbones. She could tell that he was beginning to question his belief of her betrayal and knew that she should feel in some way vindicated.

She waited for it—the slow spread of satisfaction that she had wanted so desperately in the past six months.

But it didn't come.

The flavour of victory was absent, because the only thing she could taste was Odir—a heady mix of spice and salt that turned bitter the moment she saw what lay in his eyes.

'Why didn't you tell me? What the hell was that kiss with Jarhan about?' he demanded, stepping back and thrusting his legs into the trousers he had so carelessly ripped off before.

And in an instant her heart was no longer beating with euphoria. The pressure she felt in her chest was not the same as the feel of his palm pressing between her breasts, and the confusion of the two feelings mixed within the same thought was too much to bear. *Secrets.* Years of keeping so many secrets welled within her and a familiar anxiety spread out into her lungs. She turned her head aside, unable to bear the weight of his scrutiny, slowly drawing her dress about her, covering her nakedness.

'Have you not spoken to Jarhan about it?'

'Never. The only way—the *only* way he and I could move on from that…that *night*, was to agree never to speak your name between us.'

'That is a shame,' Eloise replied, feeling the bitter sting of his familiar anger. 'It is not something that I am able to discuss.'

She pulled herself up to sit on the table and watched him pace the room.

'Discuss?'

'It is not my secret to tell, Odir,' replied Eloise, hating herself for the beseeching tone that had crept into her voice. For it was the truth. It was really *not* her secret to tell.

'And just what exactly is that supposed to mean?'

She arched an eyebrow, retreating behind the practised façade that took longer for her to assume than before. 'I am not in the habit of repeating myself, Odir.'

'I can't believe this. Even if you didn't sleep with Jarhan, you still have more loyalty to him than to your own husband!'

'Jarhan *earned* my loyalty. He spent time with me—came to see me, talked to me. He was the only person in that palace who even seemed to know or care that I was there. Your father locked himself away in his rooms, and your staff were—'

'Locked away with me,' he finished.

'Jarhan also needed someone to talk to. Together we worked on the very same outreach programme you have spent this evening lauding as if it were your own. My father and mother left Farrehed as quickly as you did after our wedding. Jarhan was my only companion.'

'This is getting us nowhere. I've explained why those two months were so difficult.'

'Yes, *today* you have. *Today* we've spoken more than in all the time we were married. Does that not strike you as odd? That it takes talk of divorce and a death to bring us together?'

The words were out of her mouth before she could recall them. But her husband didn't seem to notice.

'You can hardly claim to be innocent of what was expected of us when we married.'

'You think I had a *choice*? That I could have denied my father's demand? Did you think that it was the height of my ambitions to marry a prince?'

'Didn't have a choice? In case it hasn't escaped your notice, Eloise, this is the twenty-first century. Women have fought long and hard—burned their bras, even—so that you can have a choice. So unless you are willing to speak plainly, and stop talking in riddles, this will be a very long conversation indeed. One that, as you know, I *really* don't have time for.'

He looked at his wife, glaring at him like a hell cat. God only knew what the expression on his own face was like. He was furious, and he knew that some of that fury was misplaced towards Eloise. He was angry with himself because he was missing something. *Why* would his wife direct his questions to his brother? *Why* couldn't she just tell him?

'Secrets or silence—these are the only things that you offer me,' he bit out into the cold room.

'And all you offered me was absence!'

'Well, *habibti*,' he said, barely reining in his fury,

'I'm promising now that you will *not* be spending the rest of this marriage alone. A king needs heirs, and as we have finally proved that there is at least one area we are compatible in,' he went on, feeling once more the heat of desire tighten his body in anticipation of times to come, 'that shouldn't be such a hardship.'

He could see small shivers beginning to ripple through his wife and hated it that he had put them there—not through the stirrings of a mutual desire, but at the thought of them spending their lives together.

When had he become such a bastard that he would bind a woman to him against her will?

When the country he loved had been put in such jeopardy, that was when.

The thought, sounding so much like his father, turned his blood to ice, cutting off any delicious threads of desire in their tracks.

'I will get some food sent up. I haven't seen you eat all night.'

'You think I can eat at a time like this, Odir? Besides, it's two a.m. You can't ask the staff to bring you food now.'

'I am a king, Eloise. I can do exactly what I like.'

She watched him with grim eyes. 'Yes, and now you are sounding like one king we both once knew.'

'Have a shower, Eloise. I will call for some food.'

And with that he left the room and disappeared.

* * *

On shaky legs and bare feet Eloise silently padded through the dark room, the soles of her feet sinking into lush carpet so unlike the hard wooden floor of her little flat in Zurich. She passed through to the bedroom, ignoring the panoramic view of London because now it simply reminded her of her husband, looking out on it as if he could own the world and her with it. She looked at the thick pile of bedding that she had thought would accompany her first time with her husband, and wondered if there would ever be anything as mundane as bedding in her future.

She went through to a bathroom that would have certainly fitted her little one-bedroom apartment within its marbled walls. Silver and white clashed with black marble, exploding before her as she turned on the lights.

On autopilot, giving no heed to the fact that she was already obeying her husband's commands, she turned on the water in the shower area, stepped back, peeled the black silk dress from her body and stood there for just a moment, naked under the glare of the lighting. She presumed that somewhere there would be a dimmer switch that would transform the bathroom light into something less harsh, but Eloise welcomed the brightness. It felt as if it were burning away the darkness from her soul and her skin.

The moment the warm water touched her she sighed—an exhalation that took with it all the

thoughts of the last few hours and sent them away
from her spent body. As if the touch of the water
had brought to life all the small aches and pains that
were totally new to her body, she ran her fingers gently over the very places her husband had explored,
wondering that his touch had elicited such different
reactions from her.

Reactions that had revealed her naïve fantasies
of what it would be like to sleep with Odir to be just
that. Childish. Not in nature, but in fact. And with
the reality of what had passed between them all those
fantasies had melted away into nothing, like a passing mist covering the land and being burnt away by
the sun.

She had truly been innocent of what passed between a man and a woman. Because, had she not
been, she doubted very much that she would have
let him touch her even once. And now that she had?
Now that *he* had? She was absolutely, concretely cer-
tain that there was no going back. She might not go
forward with him—she might still find a way out of
this marriage—but there was no doubt that the events
of tonight had changed her irrevocably.

She stood beneath the spray, relishing the feel
of it because…because she was feeling something.
For the first time in years, since even before their
marriage, she was *feeling* something. Just as in the
way she had thought the desert had once brought
her to life, Odir had drawn forth a vision of herself,

powerful and desirable, from somewhere she had thought buried deep. It had been incredible, and her body still vibrated with the hum of pleasure they had shared.

She felt it strengthen her. Reshape her into someone who had perhaps started to grow in Zurich. Building on those months when she had nursed a fragile confidence into being—a confidence that perhaps had led her to this very moment.

Was it possible that they could build the marriage she had once dreamed of? That they could have a true partnership?

She allowed herself a moment to imagine it, to imagine what it would look like. But there were still things that Odir might never understand. Her reluctance to tell him the truth about Jarhan, the truth about her father and the hold he had over her mother, the truth of what no one else had ever wanted to see about the British Ambassador.

Odir let out a breath he hadn't realised that he'd been holding. He'd hung up the phone on his personal concierge what felt like hours ago, all the while straining his ears beyond the clipped English accent, waiting to hear the sounds of the shower if only simply to locate his wife within the penthouse apartment.

His wife. A woman he held such different versions of within his mind. The innocent young Englishwoman, delicate and fragile. The cheating bride who had slept with his brother. The incredible woman who had come to life in his arms. So many different façades. And tonight he had broken them all, felt, touched and tasted skin, the flesh and blood beneath it, and there was no turning back.

She had been innocent. But with that realisation came the crashing sense of dread that there were still secrets. Secrets she kept from him…secrets about his brother.

What could be so bad that Jarhan would rather he believed his wife and his brother had been together? The world tipped on its axis again, and a niggling thought about Jarhan came unbidden—one he hadn't had for years. He needed the world to stop turning. He needed to know.

He stalked through the bedroom, ignoring the stunning view, and emerged into a bathroom he hadn't yet seen. He wondered that she hadn't heard him, but realised that the sound of the shower had masked his footfalls. He was greeted by a sight that took his angry breath away.

Eloise stood beneath the cascading water, her pale skin almost merging with the white marble behind it, bearing only the faintest flush of heat to bring her to life. How could he ever have imagined her to be of the same cold, stone material lining the shower walls? How could he ever have imagined her as anything other than flesh and blood?

He watched as the water flowed over the smooth

skin of her lithe body, covering it in the way his hands and tongue had done only half an hour earlier. Need stormed through him, sending the shivers of desire that he had wanted only to inflict on *her* across his body.

He had to stop this. He couldn't allow his hunger for her to take root or he would be driven to madness.

'If you don't tell me what is going on with my brother I will call him myself and bring him here.'

She let out a cry, turning so quickly she almost slipped on the wet tiles.

Cursing, he grabbed a towel, leaned in through the water and turned it off, paying no heed to the way his shirt sucked in the warm droplets as she jerked away from the proximity of his touch, which angered him more than he could say.

'Cover yourself. I mean it. If you don't tell me what is going on I'll get Jarhan in this apartment in less than two minutes—even if Malik has to drag him here—whether you are dressed or not,' he warned, flinging the towel at her. 'Two minutes, Eloise. You have two minutes.'

And with that he stalked from the bathroom.

Eloise looked at the pool of black silk on the floor and although she didn't want to put it back on she knew that it would be better than the thick white cotton towel that barely managed to cover her thighs.

From the moment Odir had issued his command

it had taken only a second for her skin to turn from delightfully warm to ice-cool. But she wouldn't allow herself to be cowed. She would meet him as his equal.

Her regained composure threatened to dissolve when she realised that she couldn't find her thong, and she cursed the flush of desire that sprang up and painted her cheeks at the memory of how Odir had used it so effectively to bind her in a position to his liking, from where he could gain the deepest access with his tongue.

The throb at her core burst to life once more, and only now could she know that the only thing that would assuage that need was him. Her husband. Buried deeply within her until she felt nothing else— nothing but him all around her and inside her.

'I'm waiting.'

His voice cut through the room and through her desire.

She dropped the towel and stepped into the dress, pulling it over her chest and sensitised nipples, the silk fabric unusually warm from the steam of the shower.

Eloise knew that Odir wouldn't stop until he had the truth of that night. But how could she tell him? How could she trust him not to go through with what was Jarhan's greatest fear? Had Odir not already proved just how far he would go for the security of his country? Would he choose that over his brother?

She stepped into the living room, gazing around her at the sight of it, finally lit up for the first time that night. 'Luxury' was not enough to describe the surroundings she found herself in.

She cast a glance at the mountains of food that had been delivered in her absence and laughed. She couldn't help herself.

'What is so funny?' Odir asked, looking up from the stack of papers he held in one hand, the pen that was poised to strike against some unsuspecting words in the other.

'It's lobster,' she replied.

'And?'

'And I'm allergic to seafood. You would kill me before I've even had a chance to conceive those heirs you so desperately want.'

'If I'd wanted you dead, Eloise, it could have been arranged,' he said under his breath, sounding rather like a stroppy child instead of a soon-to-be king.

'I'm sure of it,' she replied in an equally droll tone. 'You used to threaten anyone in the palace with such a fate were they even to *look* as if they would refuse your command.'

'I didn't *ask* for the lobster. I just told them to bring up some food. It's not as if I don't have a million other things to be worrying about.'

'Other than me?'

'Yes, Eloise. I have a funeral to plan, a country to save, and a press briefing that is written so badly it

makes my teeth hurt. I'm afraid your dietary require-
ments are a little low down on my list of priorities.'

'Makes your teeth hurt?'

'You were the first person I told about my father's
death. In a little under six hours I am supposed to
address the world's press. And *this*,' he said, waving
the papers in the air, 'could have been written better
by my five-year-old cousin.'

Rather than the anger that had dominated his tone
in the last few hours, Eloise was surprised to find a
note of confused helplessness in his voice.

'Where is Anders? Doesn't he usually handle this
kind of thing for you?'

'Anders's wife rather inconveniently decided that
today, of all days, would be the perfect time to give
birth to their child. And whilst I may be many things,
I could not in all conscience demand that he give up
his station in the maternity wing.'

'Well, I doubt she did that on purpose.'

'You'd be surprised…. She doesn't like me much.'

'I can't imagine why,' she replied, with a great
deal of scepticism.

'What's that supposed to mean?'

'Well, given that Anders accompanied you on
every single diplomatic visit you deemed fit to make
in the two months I was at the palace, it's a wonder
she was able to get pregnant in the first place.'

All Odir could offer in response was a rather undignified grunt.

'Did you want me to look at it?' she asked, offering an olive branch.

No matter what had passed between them, what still might pass between them, he was her husband. The pain and the hurt that they'd caused each other didn't take away from the fact that once they had been close, had shared confidences. And she knew that this must be hard for him.

'Would you? You used to put together the briefings for the foundation and you were always good at…' He waved his hand in the air, as if communicating with the press was a frippery he could do without.

'Ouch, that must have hurt!' she said.

'What? Offering you a compliment?'

A smile teased the corners of her mouth. She held out her hand for the briefing and sank into one of the suite's chairs. As far away from the lobster as she could get.

She scanned the prepared speech as Odir placed a call to remove the offending foodstuffs from their suite.

'Are you hungry? I suppose someone could always call for a pizza.'

She resisted the urge to roll her eyes. 'Of course *someone* could call for a pizza. Don't worry, I'll be fine. Just give me a minute and I'll have this read.'

Odir watched Eloise, her long shapely legs hanging over the arm of the chair, bouncing up and down as she held his pen—a pen that had cost more than he was willing to admit—not so delicately between her teeth. Occasionally she retrieved it from the lips he'd spent the previous hour plundering and scored a few marks on the paper, scribbled something in the margin, then returned the pen to her teeth and carried on her perusal.

As he looked on it struck him that the scene was oddly domestic. Rather than feeling invaded, as if she'd intruded on his duties as he'd once imagined she might, he felt...*good*. It was good to have a second opinion. He could trust her in that. She certainly would not hold back—she hadn't once since she'd arrived. Until they had come to talk about Jarhan.

'I did know that you were allergic to seafood. And I hadn't actually looked at what they'd delivered.'

He didn't know what had prompted him to say such an inane thing. He just wanted her to look at him. He wanted to see the intensity of her gaze turned on him rather than the briefing.

'As you said, if you'd wanted me out of the picture... Okay. I'm done.'

'Already?'

'It wasn't *that* bad, Odir. It got a little unnecessarily wordy in the middle, and I've removed some of the repetition. Whoever wrote it...'

He felt his eyes narrow fractionally. It must have been that that tipped her off.

'*You* wrote it?' she asked with a raised eyebrow.

'Don't. I don't need to hear any more. I was the one who said it could be better.'

'Well. Like I said, it wasn't *that* bad.'

There was a glint in her eye. One that he almost didn't want to see go. But he'd meant what he'd said when he'd interrupted her in the shower. He wanted to know what was going on with Jarhan. Beneath his gaze the glint disappeared as she realised that he wasn't going to let the matter drop.

'I need to know.'

'You can't force him to tell you, Odir. It would kill him,' she said quietly, putting the papers aside on the table.

'Again with the dramatics, Eloise. If he can't tell me, then you will. Just tell me,' he commanded.

'If I tell you, then I need your promise that you will at least hear me out.'

It was on the tip of Odir's tongue to say 'no'. To refuse such a promise. But there was something in Eloise's eyes—a resolution of sorts, a determination. She was suddenly more regal than he had ever seen her and he knew—*knew*—what kind of queen she would make.

He could see the protectiveness she was showing for his brother in every line of her body. She was like a lioness, protecting her cub, and that was more than he had ever received from anyone in his living memory.

He supressed the thin spike of jealousy that pierced his chest and nodded his assent.

'I want to hear it from your lips, Odir. Say you promise or I will not say one more word.'

He bit back his frustration and the desire to let out a rather undignified growl. 'I swear it. I will not speak until you are done.'

'You were supposed to be away that night, visiting Kalaran.'

He remembered. A sandstorm had prevented them from being able to access the only road that went across the border.

'We didn't know that you had been forced to turn back. Only that you had left. After dinner, Jarhan started drinking.'

Odir frowned. 'Jarhan didn't drink back then.'

'He did that night. The reason for your visit to Kalaran was to confirm the plans your father had made for Jarhan to marry one of Prince Imin's sisters—'

'Plans that disintegrated the moment I found him with *you*.'

Eloise narrowed her eyes. By God, she was glorious like this. Cutting a king down to size was no easy feat, and she managed it with a simple glance.

'Yes. They did,' she said, as if those words contained the answer he was looking for. 'He was drunk because he didn't know what to do. He couldn't agree to the marriage you were arranging.'

'But there *was* no marriage! We didn't even know

which of Imin's sisters would be suitable for Jarhan. Why would he object to a marriage before a match had even been made?'

'Because,' she said gently, as if preparing him for some great hurt, 'it wouldn't have mattered *which* sister you chose.'

'Because he was already in love with you?' he said, hating himself for the fear that lay beneath those words. Hating the fear that clogged his breath but didn't quite stop his mouth.

'No, because it wouldn't have mattered which *woman* you chose.'

Shock cut through him and he could see the truth in her eyes.

'My brother is *gay*?'

His wife nodded.

He needed a minute. He needed a week, a month— a damned lifetime. He needed the years he had spent with his brother back.

'How could he not tell me?' he demanded.

She was shaking her head. 'It wasn't about you,' she replied.

Shame and sadness filled him. Not because his brother was gay—not at all. But because of how hard those years must have been for him. For Jarhan not to be able to be himself, not to go after the things he wanted from life. Odir knew something of that. Or at least he understood.

Odir had never been given the luxury of wanting

anything other than the throne. And to think that in his heart of hearts he had been jealous of the freedom his brother had been afforded as second son. Now he knew it to be no freedom at all. Farrehed was a deeply traditional country, and he knew how his father would have reacted to the news that Jarhan was gay. Badly. Had he been alive, he would most likely have exiled Jarhan in shame.

'Why didn't you tell me sooner? Did you think—even for one minute—that I was homophobic? That I would banish my own brother?'

There was a pause before her response—one that created the most awful ache.

'No.'

The relief he felt was like a live thing within him.

'No, it's not because of that. But we both knew that you were trying to be the best possible future ruler for Farrehed. That for you to gain the crown would have meant the ruthless pursuit of all things perfect and the utter removal of anything that would risk the throne.'

'That is not a reasonable excuse, Eloise.'

'For God's sake—you would pay me millions of pounds, tell a room full of complete strangers that I'm pregnant, all the while still being a virgin, and yet you have the audacity to be outraged by our concern about what you might do? Tell me, Odir, at what point does the end no longer justify the means?'

His answer was swift and harsh.

'At no point, Eloise. At no point does the end *not* justify the means. Do you know what's going on in my country? *Really* know? There are people in the desert tribes dying for the lack of decent medical care. Because my father withheld it in the belief that if they were weak they would not mount a counter-offensive against the throne.

'There are people in my country starving, emaciated, going hungry. Fathers are selling their daughters, husbands whoring out their wives—all because of my father, because of his delusion and paranoia.

'Destruction, a huge divide between poverty and incredible wealth, the outright sale of our country's best assets and complete isolation from its closest allies. Piece by piece my father has stripped everything from this nation, and I will do whatever I have to to see them returned. Each and every one of them!'

Eloise had seen all manner of determined men, and she knew that fire in his eyes—knew that it was not the determination of the justified, it was the determination of the desperate. It was the look of a man who would use any means necessary, never mind the cost, to get what he wanted.

'So just because what you want is for someone else—some*thing* else—it justifies any action you will take?'

'Yes.'

'I will not allow you to use either myself or Jarhan to meet such insane ends. It's a sacrifice too far.'

He wheeled round to her and closed the gap between them with two impossibly large strides.

'What the hell would *you* know about sacrifice?' His words were a harsh whisper, full of anger and accusation.

'What would I...?' she asked into the night, and all the words, all the hurt, all the pain and loneliness crept up her throat and got stuck there.

Before she realised, she'd raised her hand and slapped him. The noise echoed in the silent suite.

'Of all the things I've said to you tonight, Eloise, that is perhaps the one that least warrants such a dramatic reaction.'

'Really? What do *I* know about sacrifice? I married *you*, didn't I?'

CHAPTER EIGHT

August 2nd, 03.00-04.00, Heron Tower

SHE HAD STRUCK her husband. She had struck the Sheikh of Farrehed. She abhorred violence—abhorred abuse of any kind. Never in her life had she ever raised a hand in anger to anyone. Not until tonight.

She didn't count the pathetic punches she had peppered his chest with earlier that evening. They had been born of frustration. But what she had just done… That had been born of a fury that she had not been able to contain. The disdain, the sneer that had painted Odir's tone when he had accused her of knowing nothing of sacrifice…it had been too much to bear.

She rushed from the suite, falling into the corridor, and pushed through a heavy fire door, her feet slapping on concrete stairs until she came to the floor that had housed the charity gala and the balcony. She pulled herself up suddenly, sure that she would look like a deer caught in the headlights were anyone there to witness her.

She had forgotten the guests—forgotten the party that had been in full swing when they had left it earlier that evening. Holding her breath, and hoping to high heaven that the last of the guests had gone, she listened for any sounds to let her know one way or the other.

After the longest held breath she exhaled into the silence, finally sure that no guests had lingered.

She felt a presence behind her and knew that it wasn't her husband. She turned to find Malik standing in the shadows, in front of the fire door she had just emerged through.

'Please, Malik. I need…' She groped for a word that would convey even a fraction of what she needed at that moment, but she saw him nod.

She had never known why he had helped her all that time ago, but he had. Why he had been willing to whisk the errant Princess away from his Prince she would never know. But here he was once more, allowing her what she needed.

She left her soft *thank you* in the corridor behind her and pushed through the glass doorway, stepping out on to the balcony.

It was darker than before. The twinkling lights of London had dimmed, as if they too were hiding in shame. Once again she was struck by the sight. She had been so long away from England that she could see the beauty in it as if she was merely a visitor and hadn't been born and raised there.

She thought of all the time she had spent being dragged along on her father's diplomatic postings throughout the Arabic states. Countries where she and her mother had been installed and requested to perform. Her heart ached at the memory of those years. Her skin ached at the memory of all those false smiles.

In spite of those years Farrehed had seemed like an exotic faraway place—a desert kingdom after the three years she had spent at university in England. But instead of finding freedom in her studies, like the freedom she had tentatively come to believe that she'd found in Zurich, she had felt only a sense of postponement. A last-minute reprieve before her father's final act of dominance fell upon her.

It was there on the balcony, her mind straddling two worlds, the past and the present, that Odir found her.

'You can't keep running.'

It was testament to the hold of her memories that she had not noticed the presence of her husband before then.

She let a bitter laugh escape her lips and be carried away on the wind into the night sky. She felt a thick heavy blanket about her shoulders and sank into its warmth, not having realised how cold she was.

The sound of the outdoor heaters came from behind her as Odir's guards lit them one by one. She hated that he was so comfortable with their presence that he was ready and willing to have such a personal conversation with them present. The kind of personal conversation they should have had before she had left for Switzerland—before he had busied himself with his country's needs.

Before they were married.

She heard the sounds of the glass door sliding shut behind them and knew that they were alone.

'I want to know what you mean. About sacrifice.'

She smiled ruefully into the night air.

'I can't tell you.'

'More secrets?' he said, but this time without the sting of his previous statements.

'No. I *literally* can't tell you.'

He seemed amused by this, and somewhere deep down within her a small sense of humour—ironic humour, admittedly—rose within her. It tainted in a tone that sounded strange even to her own ears.

She shrugged. 'There's a non-disclosure agreement binding my access to my grandfather's trust fund.' She watched as her quick-minded husband absorbed this. 'My father put it on the trust the day I agreed to marry you. If I break the agreement then everything I have worked for these last six months will be for nothing. *Everything.*'

'I am your husband. I am your *King.*'

'You're above the law?' she asked.

'Yes,' he said arrogantly, as if she should have known that. 'Here, I am. And as my wife so are you.

Members of the royal household are immune from arrest in civil proceedings. Of course if you really do want that divorce then you will not be part of the royal household any more…'

He was taunting her, but not with malice. If she had not known her husband so well she might have thought there was a trace of that humour she had seen glimpses of earlier—traces of the humour that she remembered from the period of their engagement.

But still, she wondered if Odir was right. Perhaps, once again, she had simply taken her father's words as the truth, as gospel. Perhaps her father had known that she wouldn't question it. Had it only been a piece of paper that she had signed, she might more easily have given in. But it wasn't. It was the promise she had made to her mother.

'I don't like to break my promises,' she said.

'But what of the promise you made to *me*?'

'It's not that easy, Odir.'

She had not once spoken about her family. To anyone. But the choice not to speak now wasn't out of habit—it was about so much more than that.

'How do I know you won't use this against me to get what you want? To keep me by your side?'

'Is that not sacrifice? To give up something for someone else?'

'No,' she argued. 'It's not about sacrifice. It's about giving away a piece of my soul to a man who views love as something to be feared, something to be avoided at all costs.'

'Love makes you weak, Eloise. Perhaps you know something of that?'

'I know that it's a sentiment you hold about you as if it were your very last defence. But I'm not so sure that you are right about it.'

She looked at her husband through the veil of secrets that had built up between them—some her fault, some his—and even though they disagreed she began to feel as if there *was* something between them. Something woven in the darkness of this night. Something that had been missing from their interaction even during their engagement.

Odir might be slightly misguided—zealous even—in his pursuit of ensuring the success of his country, but she knew, despite her accusations, that he was an honourable man. And, despite what he thought, he *did* love his people, he *did* love his country. He loved his brother, too, or he would have turned his back on Jarhan the moment he'd thought him guilty of pursuing his wife, or the moment he'd discovered his brother's secret.

He was bound by love in every decision he made, in every act he did for his country. What would it be like to have that turned on *her*? Turned in her favour, for once?

Without realising it, Eloise had conjured up another image of what their marriage might have been like—could *be* like now.

Her mind flew ahead through the years to see a marriage that was born of truth, honesty and love. Half torn between the present and an impossible future, she felt her heart leap and plummet at the same time, seesawing within her until she felt completely lost.

Her husband—the one in the present, not the one of her momentary fantasy—shifted in the night before her, and Eloise knew that if she didn't take this first step—if she didn't reach out for the future that she could see within her heart—then it would never happen. She would never have the love and the security she had spent a lifetime searching for.

But to share her greatest secret—one that was almost a part of her, as if she had been born with it, rather than before it—was a risk. If her father found out she would never get her inheritance and be able to help Natalia and all those the medical centre helped. And if her husband turned his back on her then she would be left with nothing.

'Is that not sacrifice? To give up something for someone else?'

Odir watched as Eloise seemed to sag under the weight of a decision made, and he felt a stirring of satisfaction settle over his body as he knew one more secret was about to dissolve between them. Knew they were taking one more step together towards an agreement, towards the press conference. Towards everything he had wanted at the beginning of this day.

'I can see how many people would think that I had lived a charmed life. My ambassador father... stationed in exotic places all over the world. Living a life full of money, security. I suppose some would even consider it glamorous. The first place I remember living was Bahrain. My memories are full of sunlight and white walls. I had a British nanny who came with us when my father was next stationed in Oman.'

Odir frowned, wondering if the controlling man he had first met had been indiscreet with one of his staff. That would account for the ridiculous legal binding he'd placed on his daughter's trust fund. None of the countries surrounding Farrehed would put up with an ambassador so indiscreet.

Eloise had picked up on his thoughts.

'No, it wasn't a taste for young British nannies that defined my father. More a taste for oil-rich countries. I'm pretty sure that it still eats at him that he was never sent to the UAE.'

A small smile spread across her dark features, and Odir realised that Eloise was perversely happy about that.

'He has the temperament for it, you see. Negotiation, confidence, a winning personality... And he's able to exert his influence and will over others. He's good at that. He consumes information at a rate of knots and excels at reading between the lines. A British ambassador once said you need "a quick mind, a hard head, a strong stomach, a warm smile and a cold eye" to deal in such countries. He has all that in spades.'

'You don't sound as if you admire those qualities.'

'How can I when they were used against his own family? Used solely to get what he wanted and damn the consequences for anyone else.'

Eloise had never been a selfish person, and with hindsight Odir could see the holes in his belief that she had been unfaithful, that she was motivated purely by money. And he began to think that she wasn't talking only about herself.

'And your mother?' he asked, putting his quick thinking to the test.

'Yes. It was particularly hard for her.'

The tenor of her voice changed, began to unravel, as did the wall of secrecy around her family.

'She was—is still—a beautiful woman. According to my father, they met at university, fell in love. It was a full Cinderella story, only in reverse. My mother was the youngest daughter in a crumbling old aristocratic family. And, whilst the hereditary peerage would go to her brother, my father had still married into minor British aristocracy. Not too bad for a boy from Coventry.'

At Odir's apparent shock, she continued.

'Oh, yes—as the son of a civil servant, he made it good.'

Her voice was cold and cynical, with no trace of pride whatsoever.

'I believe my mother fell hard for him. He's a very charming man when he wants to be.'

'And when he doesn't?'

'He's cold, ruthless, manipulative, and he will do absolutely anything it takes to get his hands on what he wants. '

Odir realised then that he had never really known why she had agreed to marry him. That he'd been so focused on what she could bring to *him*, what good he could do with her connections to the British establishment, that he had simply assumed she was in agreement.

'Including selling his daughter for the connections to royalty it would bring. The deals he could make once his daughter was married to the Sheikh of Farrehed.'

Her words matched his own thoughts so closely that he felt something horribly like shame rise within him.

'You could have said no.'

'Not really. My mother didn't adapt that well to the climate of the Middle East. Oh, she enjoyed the parties, the social gatherings. But, contrary to popular opinion, they don't happen every night. My father left her alone for long periods of time, and without friends, without that crumbling aristocratic family she had left in England, she was confined to a life of boredom and solitude.'

Like I gave to you… The thought erupted in Odir's mind.

'But instead of finding something to do, making something of her life without him, she sought escapism. Nothing so uncouth as alcohol, but pills. Lots and lots of mother's little helpers. Not that she was much of a mother. Not really,' she said sadly. 'In each placement I would be sent to English-speaking schools, often boarding rather than being a day student.

'I don't think I really noticed anything until the summer when I was about fourteen. My father was off attending the petroleum conferences, and my mother… Meal times were the worst. Watching her shuffle food that she had no stomach for around a plate. The sound of cutlery scratching against china still sends shivers through me.

'I tried to find things for us to do together, but she wasn't really in a fit state during the day. She'd spend a lot of time in her bed. At first I thought she was ill. But then, when she was high, she'd be overly bright…false and forced laughter would echo through the halls. But through that cracked, jangly exuberance would be a thread of neediness, a constant search for reassurance that…' she shook her head in shame '…that I despised. That I was embarrassed by.'

Shame and guilt warred within Eloise. She hated herself for that. For sharing emotion with her father and feeling embarrassed about her mother. Hated to think that she was anything like him.

'I went back to the UK for university and plunged myself into my studies. I thought I was being a good student, but in reality I was just hiding. In Zurich, working at the medical centre, I learned of the psychological effects both before and after addiction had taken hold. I began to see why my mother had turned to pills, given her life with her husband, given my father… I began to wonder if there was something I could have done if I'd been present…if I'd been allowed to be.'

The helplessness in her voice took hold of something deep within Odir. It echoed within a bruised heart he would have denied to any other living soul.

Slowly things began to fall into place in Odir's mind. Those painful dinner conversations at the palace, when her mother's pale, drawn face and her almost constant silence had been so at odds with her daughter's desperate attempts to take the focus from her, to fill the silence, to be the plaster over a wound so deep and infected with hatred.

'When I came to Farrehed after university I confronted my father about it—about why he didn't force her to get help. He said she was beyond help. I threatened to take her away, and that's when he showed me the videos. He'd recorded them on his camera.

Times that even I hadn't seen her. Erratic, horrible, slurring… She was…she was like a wounded animal. Begging my father for pills, screaming at housekeepers. Raving at imaginary slights from strangers.'

Images rushed through Eloise's mind—blurry, jerky images placed there by numerous videos, captured for posterity by a father who would blackmail his own child. Hatred and despair warred within her.

'He threatened to cut her off, to go to the press and publicly denounce his "druggy wife". He said that he'd sever her financial support under the guise of cutting off her access to drugs, but that he would really just leave her to the mercy of the health service.

'I didn't think he'd do it. Ruin his own reputation just to get what he wanted. But he insisted that he'd ride the tidal wave of public opinion as the poor, put-upon husband who had tried to protect his wife's shame. He would be seen as a man who had done all he could to help his wife, but who couldn't take the heartbreak of it any more. He was convincing. I'll give him that.

'I still said no. I went to see my mother. To beg her to leave my father. To come with me, away from it all. I knew that I could provide for us when I got my trust fund, that we just had a few years before then. But she wouldn't leave him.

'She begged me. Begged me to keep her secret. Begged me to marry *you*.'

Her mother's hysteria that day had been terrible.

She had been wailing, begging, pleading, all of it edged with a very real fear of being cut off from the one thing she loved more than herself, more than her daughter. *Drugs*.

'So I agreed. And I agreed to the gagging order that would prevent me from talking about my mother's dirty little secret. To keep my mother happy. To get my father what he wanted.'

Odir took it all in, repositioning this new information over the family who had attended state dinners, shared private meals with his own family. This background information was filling in questions he hadn't realised he'd asked himself about the tension, the slightly odd behaviour of his mother-in-law. Her father had been relocated to Kuwait after their marriage, and Odir realised that the wedding was the last time he'd seen her father and mother.

'So you wanted to use your trust fund…?'

'Not for my mother. No, she's still with my father. After I left Farrehed I went to stay with a university friend. She had always been so understanding about my mother. About my family. I hadn't realised why at the time, but when I arrived in Switzerland I saw she had her own addiction troubles. Her family had cut her off, and to be honest she was in a much worse place than I was.

'I wanted to get her help—the kind of help that my mother had refused—but to do so I needed money. Zurich has an amazing medical centre, specialising in addiction. But by the time Natalia was admitted the damage was done. She needs a kidney transplant, but because of her addictions she's very low down on the transplant list. In the time I spent at the facility I got to know the staff, and when they were looking for an assistant to the Chief Financial Officer I applied and got the job.'

Eloise smiled ruefully.

'Yes, your very royal wife has been working as a secretary for the last six months.' A small laugh escaped her as she shared the oddity of the situation. 'But tomorrow,' she continued, and he almost flinched as her hand reached out to touch his arm, 'tomorrow, when I have access to my trust fund, I can use it to help Natalia. To help the medical centre in Zurich that will most likely close within the year if it doesn't have a large injection of capital. I was never after money or social standing, Odir...' Her voice was almost painfully earnest. 'I just wanted to...'

'Help your mother? Help your friend? After helping my brother?'

He bit back the curse that came so easily to his tongue. A tongue laced with the taste of bitterness and fury.

'Why didn't you *tell* me?' he demanded.

He thought of all the things he could have done to help—all of the ways he could have made it easier for Eloise.

'Because you had a country to run.'

It hurt that she was right.

'Because I didn't know if you would even care. In spite of the closeness we had before our wedding, and the tentative relationship we built, I didn't know if it was strong enough for the truth. And all the while I could never know what my father would do if he found out. If he had made good on the threat of the gagging order then my trust fund would have been gone and I wouldn't have been able to help anyone. If the truth had come out the promise I made to my mother to protect her, to keep my family's secret, would have burnt away to nothing. As sad as it sounds, Odir, I never had my father's love. But to lose my mother's would have been—'

He hadn't realised it, but he'd put his hands up to ward off her words. To prevent them from coming out of her mouth and hitting him like the bullets they were. Because, of all people, he knew what it was to lose a mother's love. He knew the deep, searing pain that, once felt, changed a heart irrevocably.

But to lose it by choice—to have someone choose a husband over a child, a secret over the truth—that was a different kind of pain all together. His mother's death had taken away that love for him, but that had not been a choice she had made.

'Right now, Odir, I'm trusting that you will say nothing of this to anyone, will do nothing—because it will put Natalia at risk. Put my mother at risk.'

Odir couldn't stand the weight of Eloise's gaze,

full of expectation and hope, he realised reluctantly. His mind was hurtling over all this information and it was changing his thoughts of her, refocusing the image he had carried with him over the last six months. One that had changed that fateful night he'd found her beneath Jarhan's kiss.

Now the memory was reforming into something new. His image of her slight frame, one that he had once thought weak and inconsequential, was now, he realised, of the strongest steel. One that had borne his awful accusations—one that had suffered so much at the hands of the people who were meant to protect her and care for her: her father, her mother... even her husband.

She had borne so much and never once buckled. She'd done what she had needed to do and he admired that. He respected that. It was a strength that he had not seen in anyone else around him.

She had trusted him with her secrets. Within him he could feel this new image of her shifting the synapses in his brain, bringing new weight to his feelings for her. And suddenly to have her trust felt like a burden greater than any he'd ever carried before. Not his kingdom, not his people, but this slip of a woman and her trust were threatening to undo him.

'I have money that I would willingly have given you to protect your mother and your friend.'

'But would you have listened to me six months ago? When you thought me someone who could sleep with your brother? Would you have listened to me six hours ago, when you believed me a gold-digger out for a marriage of convenience to a prince?'

His silence spoke volumes, and it hurt her more than Eloise could have anticipated. She turned away, unable and unwilling to bear the weight of it any more, and almost stumbled over the cushioned bench beside the heater that Odir's guard had lit earlier.

No, the silence seemed to say to her. They both knew that it would have been impossible before. It had all been such a mess. And all because of their fathers. They might have been very different types of tyrants, but it had still been tyranny.

Either way, Eloise realised, there was no peace to be had from either man. Odir's father was dead, and her father would not change. He would not suddenly become a kind man who would sacrifice his own wants for his family. He would not suddenly become a loving man who would protect her mother, or even her. Money, reputation, social standing—that was everything to him. And to admit to his wife's addiction…it just wouldn't happen.

She felt Odir sit down heavily beside her. There they were. Two people stripped of everything—not King nor Queen, not a son, nor a daughter. It was just the two of them, looking out at the distance, lost in their own thoughts under the night sky.

And she *wanted* to be lost. She wanted to feel

anything other than what was warring within her heart. She hated all this talk of the past, all the dirty little secrets that had kept them locked away from each other, making it almost impossible for them to be together.

She could feel the warmth from his skin across the small distance between them. The scent so uniquely his that she could have recognised it anywhere hit her in waves. She inhaled it, holding it within her lungs, trapping it inside her and refusing to let it go. She wanted it to fill her completely, to block out any thoughts of what had been spoken of, any thoughts of what was to come.

Her mind hurt from all the plans, all the scheming, all the different possibilities of where this night could have gone and would go now. She wanted him. She needed him to take it all away and fill her with the simplicity of a desire that was already stoking its flames within her.

The air changed, and she couldn't tell if it was her fault or his. She could hear her breathing—loud in her mind, full and quick—and struggled to slow it. She fought it because she knew that even just one more touch from Odir would turn those flames into an inferno.

Never before had she experienced desire like this. Oh, she had wanted him before their marriage—she had lusted after him. But now that she knew where that desire led...now that she knew what could happen between them…it was enough to make her heart explode within her chest.

'Eloise…'

He spoke her name as if it were a warning. As if it were a promise.

'Make me forget. Just for now, Odir. The morning will come, but not yet. So for now…please.'

She hated the way her voice begged him. She hated the helplessness it made her feel. She hated that she feared he would refuse her request. It was a fear so much greater than she could ever have imagined.

Odir shifted on the bench and pulled her back against his chest. He was bewitched by her. Somehow she had done something to him—something that called to his every sense, that dragged him back from dark thoughts and turned him towards an impossible desire. His arousal was quick and hard, and he knew there was no way he could stop the avalanche of need crashing through his body.

'One day, *habibti*,' he managed to grind out. 'One day I will take you to a proper bed. But right now I just can't.'

She lay between his legs, her slim pale shoulders just close enough for him to press kisses on skin bare of the black material that gathered around her neck. He thrust his tongue out to taste her, clean and fresh from the shower. There was no perfume, no flavour of anything but her in his mouth, and he wanted more.

He gathered her hands in front of her and ran his open palms up her toned arms, spreading his thumbs out to feel the swell of her breasts, and she shivered in his hold, pressing down against his erection. He pressed his hips upwards against her. God, she was going to kill him.

He flattened his palms against the sides of her breasts and pushed, passing the pads of his thumbs over her hard nipples visible through the thin silk fabric, and he thanked every god that anyone had ever prayed to that she wasn't wearing a bra.

She twisted in his arms, her mouth seeking his, but he pulled his lips away from her reach and almost laughed at the sound of her frustrated growl. Once again she reminded him of a tigress—powerful and feline, her every move a sensual delight—and he was teasing them both.

He ran his hands across the silk covering the flat of her breastbone, sliding them further to the juncture of her thighs, relishing in the warmth between her legs, gathering the fabric beneath his hands as he pressed down.

Enough. He wanted his skin on hers. He reached beneath her slender neck and released the halter neck of the dress, baring her breasts to the night sky. In the shadows her pale skin shone like marble, but it held none of the qualities of that cool stone. Eloise was flesh and blood and he wanted it all.

He caressed her breasts, skin on skin, the heat

of his hands against her cooling skin enough to drive him mad—just as mad as he was driving her. She arched her back, thrusting her small but perfect breasts into his palms. Her legs were restless against his and he knew what she was searching for.

He gathered the skirts up around her waist, felt her long, shapely thighs pressing outwards against his and nearly lost his breath. She wasn't wearing the thong that he had enjoyed so greatly before, she was naked, and he knew in that instant, just as he had known earlier, that nothing would prevent him from taking her.

He slid a finger into the blond curls between her thighs and her groan of need floated on the night air. He played with her, his fingers delighting over the small bundle of nerves at her core, her gasps like music to his ears. Again and again her need was a vocal thing, encouraging him further.

He had never seen a woman like this, glorious and lost within the world of sensation that he was providing. He had never thought that pleasing a woman could be more pleasurable than seeking his own, but he had been wrong. This was truly and singularly the most erotic thing he had ever experienced. His wife—Eloise—was the most stunningly sensual creature, and it was his name on her lips. Over and over again, pleading, begging, needing.

Her body was taut, every muscle, every line of her poised on the brink of climax, and he had the power to give her that. He withdrew his hand, preventing her from disappearing over the edge, and smiled into her neck as she growled her frustration once again. He revelled in the control he had over her, wanting to take her to the brink again and again, wanting her completely mindless, as she had requested.

If that made him a bastard, so be it. But then she did something that made him realise, once again, that he should not ever underestimate his wife...

The moment he withdrew his hand Eloise knew that he was playing with her. Not that he wouldn't make good on his sensual promise—no, she knew that would come to pass. Only he would make her pay for it first.

Gritting her teeth against the frustration soaring through her, she realised that two could play that game.

She knew that he liked to hear her—could feel the pleasure that sprang through him with each sound that left her lips. In her heart of hearts she admitted that the sound of her own desire was something that also inflamed her. She might have been a virgin only a few hours ago, but she was a quick study. He had taught her to be.

She reached beneath her, then paused, wondering—just for a moment—if she could do this...if she was ready to take control over their sensual power-play.

The way that Odir's body stilled completely beneath hers was all the answer she needed. With her back still flush against his chest she undid the clasps of his trousers beneath her, her fingers gliding the zip down, and she felt the hardness of his arousal on the backs of her hands.

He growled, the sound of his voice shockingly deep and powerful in contrast to her own. She felt his hand move back between her legs and she swatted it away. It was his turn now.

She wrapped her small hand around his hard length and revelled in the silky smoothness of his skin. The weight of him in her palm felt incredible as she gently squeezed, tightening her hold on him. She guided her hand down his length and back up again, and was surprised by the desire to taste him. To take him into her mouth.

Anticipation fired through her, but she put all thoughts of that aside. That was for another time. She focused on the feel of him, hot and hard, felt his hips flexing just as her own had moments before.

She smiled as Odir burst into Arabic, his words so quick and fast that she could only grasp the sentiment, the promise of the things he would do to her settling over her skin and into her heart. Wicked things he promised, but the warnings and threats all came to a halt suddenly with the gasp of pure need she felt echoing within her.

Suddenly he shifted beneath her. She felt his hand wrap around her own, guiding her up and down his length. His pleasure was hers, the erratic beating of his heart matching time beneath her own.

Then his hands moved again, his palms beneath her bottom lifting her just a little. She moved to grip his strong, powerful thighs, leaning forward to stay on top as he guided the head of his penis between her legs and into her from beneath. Her own slick wetness was a shock to her as he pulled her down onto his length and filled her completely. Her breath was expelled from her body as if to make room for him within her.

Trust, need and desire whipped around them, stronger than any gale force wind, binding them to each other. She pushed forward, feeling the weight of him pressing against her, causing a shock of urgent need, and it was all she could do to hold on as he thrust upwards again and again, strong and sure. One hand came around her chest, moulding her breasts, teasing her nipples, the other was back between her legs, toying with her sensitive flesh, pushing her towards the abyss that waited for her.

She couldn't hold all the sensations within her. She dragged in air to lungs so full with passion that she didn't think she could take any more. She clung desperately to the edge, fearful of losing herself, fearful of everything. Again and again he thrust into her, completely surrounding her, covering every single sensitive point of her body, and inside she was crying out for release.

'I've got you,' he whispered into her ear, his own breathing ragged but his voice steady and confident. 'I've got you. You can let go.'

For a moment her heart struggled—she didn't *want* to trust him—but her body paid no heed to her heart. The command he issued was so sure, the need he mastered so strong, that with one final powerful, incredible thrust he pushed her into an abyss of stars.

CHAPTER NINE

IT WAS THE chimes from Big Ben at the Houses of
Parliament, further down the river, that brought
Odir back from his sensual haze with an ice-cold
certainty of what was to come. He counted each
toll to four and then cursed out loud. He had just
as many hours again until the press conference and
it left a bitter taste in his mouth, washing away the
flavour of pleasure that had been there only seconds before.

It had been a moment stolen from time, as simple as a man and a woman coming together in sheer
passion, with no thought to anything else. But they
weren't just a man and a woman. They were King
and Queen. And what they had just shared was the
last moment of its kind that he could afford to take.

He was now the ruler of a country, he was now
the Sheikh. And that had to be—could only be—his
one priority. But the events of the last few hours—

the revelations he'd uncovered about his wife—made him wonder what kind of ruler he would be.

For so long he had been safe and secure in the knowledge that he would be so much better than his father. Guilt and grief sliced through him at the thought, but he couldn't allow that to overtake him. With his father gone, he now stood alone. But the doubt that had been held at bay for so long was creeping in through his carefully constructed barriers.

He had been a truly awful brother, ignoring what had been plain to see, what his wife had seen and known. He had been a terrible husband, failing to ask the questions that would have resolved so much between them, failing to support and protect his wife.

Protect his wife.

The words rang through him with a completely different meaning. It was the second time that night that they hadn't used protection and Eloise might be pregnant with his child.

The realisation was truly sobering, and the image of a small child with his dark skin and her blue eyes sprang into his mind and lodged itself into his heart. Along with the desire and need to be better than his father—more than a distant, commanding figure shaping a small child, paving over the secret wants and wishes contained in that child's heart and moulding him into being something else, *someone* else... He wouldn't be that person. He would never be like his father.

Again guilt and sorrow poured salt on to a painful open wound. He had long ago grieved for the man who had once shown him love, for the loss of his mother, and the moment he had realised that his father was human, was fallible, had faults… That was the moment Odir had truly become a man.

He never wanted his child to feel that same crashing sensation. Oh, it would happen, he was sure— Odir was not arrogant enough to think himself perfect. But still…

His father had chosen to indulge in pain, zealousness and misery. He had taken the love he had once felt for his wife and children and turned it into something bitter and damaging. And Odir knew that his country wouldn't survive if it suffered the same again. Odir would never willingly allow that threat to his people. But deep down he knew it wasn't just his people he was protecting. It was himself.

So within his mind he slowly began to rebuild the walls around his heart—brick by brick, second by second—until everything that had been undone by Eloise in the last two hours was erased. No matter what happened after tonight—no matter what happened in the next few weeks and months—he had to make sure that his feelings for Eloise were not something that would risk the future of his country…the future of his heart.

But before he could speak to Eloise of the future he had one last thing to say about the past—words that were now bursting from his chest.

'Eloise, I'm so sorry. For what I said to you earlier this evening. For what I thought of you.'

'We never really had a chance, did we?' she said, her sad smile offering sympathy, offering understanding.

'But we do *now*. We can make a go of it now. I will help you maintain Natalia's medical care. I will do whatever I can to help your mother in whatever way you want.'

Still lying on top of him, Eloise felt his breath against her neck, heard the words that he whispered into her ear, and wrapped herself in this new vow he was making to her. His apology soothed the sting of the past and she knew that he meant it. She knew that for the first time in her entire life there was someone to share her burden. To share her fear and the weight of the responsibility she had borne for so long.

'But Eloise, I can give you nothing more than that.'

He paused as if to let his words sink in. As if to allow her time to hear the truth falling from his lips.

'I cannot give you love. You were right—I *do* know how to love, I can and I have. But my love has now gone to my people. All of it. I have none left to give you.'

It hurt. More than she had ever thought it would. Her stomach cramped and she was surprised that her body didn't curl in on itself the way she wanted it so desperately to do.

Here in his arms, with his body beneath her, she felt a part of the past break away and disappear into the night. And with it came the realisation that in the last six months of trying to ensure her friend's safety she had experienced the very freedom that she had always yearned for.

Yes, she could walk away now—she could leave. If Odir wanted he could tell her father where to find her, could tell him that she had broken her promise to him and to her mother. Not that she thought he would... She could leave it all behind. But what would happen to Farrehed? What would happen to Odir?

When she had agreed to the marriage her father had arranged with Odir she had thought he might rescue her. When she'd realised that wasn't the case she had tried to make the best of it. When he had thrown her aside she had taken the opportunity and run. She had protected her friend and lived a lie for six months.

Looking back, Eloise realised that at each turn, with every step, she had been thinking only of herself. She had not thought of the man she'd married. She had not thought of the people who had become *her* people.

If she was willing—if she could put aside her own broken heart and step back into the world of royal responsibility—then she could ensure the future and the security of everyone she cared for. How on earth could she put her own wishes above all that? And if in the last few hours Odir had managed to uncover a want that she had never known she had—a want for someone, anyone, to love her for who she was and not for what she could do or what she could be— well, that wasn't his fault.

She shut her ears against the echo of a childlike voice, one from a distant memory, broken with tears, that was still asking to be loved.

Confused and hurt, desperate to reach out and comfort her past self and her future self, assuring both that one day they would all be okay, Eloise fought within herself. She had proved to herself that she was stronger than she had ever thought. She had started over again in a new country under a different identity. But in all that time there had been one thing missing from her life. And she realised now that it had been her husband.

If she decided to return to him desperately hoping that one day he'd love her the way he loved his people, she would never forgive herself. Because, no matter how weak and needy that part of her heart was, she would *never* be like her mother. But if she chose to return to Odir's side simply to protect her friend, with the hope that she might one day be able to protect her mother and protect the people of their country...

'Eloise—'

'I understand,' she interrupted.

'You agree to become my wife? To be Queen of

my country and mother to my children? You agree to all that?'

She inhaled—pressing her feet to the floor and drawing strength from the solid wood beneath her toes—and exhaled the words Odir longed to hear.

'I agree.'

For the first time in what seemed like an age Odir felt the true flush of complete victory rush through him. It was in no way nearly as powerful as the heights of pleasure that had coursed through his veins as he had found completion within her, but it was no less important.

He told himself that he hadn't recognised the way her eyes had dimmed as she'd said the words. He told himself that he'd imagined he had seen that same look in her eyes when he'd left her alone on their wedding night. He supressed the twinge that had tightened around his heart—a twinge that felt oddly like guilt—and instead made his quick mind fly to what had to happen next.

They needed to get to the embassy for the press conference so that he could become the powerful ruler his people really needed. They didn't have much time.

He stood up from the bench, holding his hand out to her, and felt the warmth eaten away by the cool touch of her skin. He brought her to her feet and they left the balcony, the past, and all the words and kisses they had exchanged behind them.

He glanced again at his watch as they silently walked to the corridor where the lift would take them to the suite. Malik was standing in the shadows, watching them from under hooded eyes. Odir bit down against what felt a little like censure coming off his guard in waves.

'Arrange for the limo to meet us downstairs in twenty minutes.'

Malik's silent nod poked again at his conscience—as did his wife's bowed head, reflected over and over and over again in the mirror-lined lift. He fought against the urge to lift her chin and see into the azure depths of her eyes—eyes that would tell him what was going on in her mind. There was a secret, cowardly part of him that didn't want to know.

They entered the suite and Eloise pulled up short.

'What is it?'

'Your bags. They've been packed.'

'Of course.'

'You *knew* I would agree?'

The hurt and the accusation in the eyes he'd wanted to see only moments before cut through him now like a knife.

'Yes,' he said simply.

Because he couldn't deny it. There had been no other acceptable outcome from this evening.

He watched her gaze run over the room, taking in

the fact that all the signs of their lovemaking, all the signs of the chaos they had lost themselves to, had been erased. A delicate blush came to her cheeks and he watched her realise that some unseen hand had wiped away the traces of their passion and returned the room to its previous state.

'When will I be able to see Natalia? There are things I need to finish up in Zurich.'

Her question surprised him. The intrusion of the life that she had left him for was strangely unwelcome to him.

'Soon. I will look into having Natalia brought to Farrehed for the best medical treatment available.'

He watched a crease appear between her delicate brows.

'Habibti?'

'Natalia needs a kidney transplant. And I'm not sure that taking her away from possible matches would be for the best right now... I don't suppose you'd let me return to Switzerland before coming to Farrehed?'

'I need you, Eloise.'

The timbre of his voice sent shivers into her heart, made her tremble with hope—until he finished his sentence.

'You will need to be by my side as much as possible, especially in these first few months.'

'Then Natalia should stay in Switzerland until

after a transplant can be done. Odir, I'm telling you now that when that happens I *will* be by her side.'

He clearly saw the determination she channelled into her gaze, her voice, and nodded his acceptance.

'No matter what political or royal appointment it might interrupt?'

'No matter what. Eloise, your friend is important to you—I understand that.'

Just not enough for her to be allowed to say good-bye Eloise thought sadly.

But Natalia would understand. While they had been in Switzerland she and Natalia had spoken often of Odir. After two months Natalia had stopped urging her to speak to the husband that Natalia had never met.

Once again Eloise found herself wondering how—in spite of the awful treatment from her own fiancé and the painful abandonment of her family—Natalia had retained such an optimistic hope that everything would be all right in the end.

'I'm going to have a shower,' Odir said, his words cutting through her thoughts. 'Is there anything you need to do to prepare for your return?'

'My boss knew that I would be away for at least a week. I arranged for one of the other PAs to cover in my absence. I can get in touch with him later and let him know. But I should call my mother. Even if she doesn't see the press conference, word will reach her soon enough.'

A decisive nod of his proud dark head was Odir's only reaction as he padded through to the bedroom.

It would be around seven in the morning in Kuwait, so hopefully she wouldn't have to wake her mother. She dialled the number at her parents' current posting, knowing that her father wouldn't answer the phone. Her parents still slept in separate rooms, and Eloise felt safe in the knowledge that she could have a conversation with her mother unhindered by his presence. She just hoped that her mother would be sober enough to listen…

The sound of the ringing through the phone line felt uncomfortably loud in her head.

'Hello?'

Her mother's voice sounded uniquely absent of sleep and drugs, and Eloise's heart clenched at the thought that her mother might have somehow been expecting her call.

'Hi, Mum,' she replied.

'Oh, it is you. Your fath— David has been all over the place, announcing his royal grandchild to anyone who would listen.'

For a moment Eloise was utterly confused. And then the events from hours before came flooding back, and she could hardly credit that the news had got out so quickly.

'Mum, there's no—'

'He's so happy, Eloise. Honestly, I can't thank you enough.'

A stinging burn of acid hit the back of her throat to hear her mother's happiness at Odir's lie. She pushed down the familiar, impotent anger that rose within her whenever her mother illustrated just how dependent she was on her husband's good mood. She wanted to reach through the phone and shake some sense into the older woman, but knew it would do no good.

For the first time that evening she had sympathy for Odir, who saw love as a weakness, as a destructive, hurtful thing. He didn't realise that it was the person who wielded love that caused such weakness. Not the emotion itself.

'I told Odir. About everything.'

She felt her mother's silence as if it were a shout.

'It's okay, Mum. He's promised not to say anything to anyone. I know I promised you that I wouldn't tell anyone, but keeping a secret from my husband… Mum, it's a promise I couldn't keep.'

The silence from the other end of the phone was white-hot. Eloise held her breath, realising that even now she couldn't predict how her mother would react. Whether she would be angry…whether she would break down.

'You could come with me, Mum,' Eloise said.

She might not have asked Odir, but she knew he'd allow it—make it happen if he could. Again, that small part of herself that hoped her mother would choose *her* this time—would choose her over the drugs, over her husband—raised its head. 'You could leave him and—'

'No. I… It's my whole life, Eloise. I know what I'm doing here. With David. He needs me. If I were to come to Farrehed everything would be different. I wouldn't know where to start. I wouldn't know how to…'

Wouldn't know how to be the mother that she needed, Eloise realised. Her mother didn't know how to be that, and nor did she have the strength to *try* to be that. Angelina Harris's addiction was too strong for her to choose a difficult path. To choose her daughter and leave her husband.

'I'm getting help. Here. I am. I *am,* Eloise. But I need to do it here.'

Without you, Eloise finished in her mind.

Not for the first time she hoped that her mother was telling the truth, but this time, as if looking at her mother from a distance, she viewed her words with another meaning. Her mother was making her own kind of sacrifice and it was the only thing her mother's kind of love made her capable of. To let Eloise go. To let her be free of the responsibility of her mother.

'I hope that you will visit one day, Mum. But I'm saying this now—David will not set one foot in Farrehed.'

Another silence—and yet this time it was a settled one. An accord between mother and daughter.

'I understand,' her mother replied.

They said their goodbyes, and Eloise wondered when or even *if* she would see her mother again.

She looked up to see Odir standing in the bed-room doorway, his frame illuminated from behind, casting his face in shadow.

'How much did you hear?' Eloise asked, unable to discern his features.

'Enough.'

'I hope that I wasn't being presumptuous—about my father.'

'If you hadn't said it, *habibti,* I would have,' he replied.

His words sent a ripple of satisfaction and right-ness into the hurt, cold part of her, warming her just a little. A sad smile played on her lips as she passed him on her way to the bathroom.

In less than ten minutes she had showered and dressed, redone her make-up and hair as best she could. All the while trying not to acknowledge the depth of feelings in her heart.

She emerged from the bathroom and entered the suite to find Odir waiting for her.

'The limo is here.'

Odir was holding out his hand and she knew that she must take it. That it was time to accept her re-sponsibilities just as Odir accepted his.

Perhaps they were not so different from each other after all.

CHAPTER TEN

August 2nd, 05.00-06.00, Farrehed Embassy

ELOISE PEERED THROUGH the blacked-out windows of the luxurious limo that glided through the quiet streets. The last time she had been out in London had been years ago, when she and Natalia had celebrated the end of university. Then the city had been packed full of drunk revellers, pouring out of nightclubs, but now bulletproof tinted glass protected her from roads empty save for cleaners and refuse collectors.

London felt a million miles away from Farrehed. The dark stone slabs of Fleet Street rose up about them—so different from the bright sandstone of Hathren, Farrehed's main city. And equally different from the neat, structured streets of Zurich.

Eloise felt a strange, unworldly nostalgia rise within her. Something that spoke of home. Or was it simply because beside her in the limo was the solid, silent presence of her husband? She couldn't tell any more. She was so very tired. They both were.

The silence between them filled up all the space in the elegant car, all the space in her heart.

Odir watched Eloise, her face pressed up against the glass like a child taking in new sights. There was something different about her now. That evening she had not been the woman he'd married. He wondered once again that he had ever thought her to be made of porcelain, made of a shell that held nothing beneath it other than cold calculation.

When she had first entered the room at Heron Tower she had been filled with energy, determination. It had vibrated under her skin, lending it a rosy colour that alluded to life, to fire and passion. But now... Now she was somewhere in between. The cool pallor of her skin was nothing like the fine white marble that filled the halls of the palace in Farrehed, but it was also something very different from the soft and smooth warm silk he knew she *could* feel like.

It was as if she had lost something—withdrawn from him somehow—and he didn't like it. Odir hated silence at the best of times, but right now it reminded him of the shroud that had descended over the palace after his mother's death. As if all the life and the energy of the country had died with her.

'The press conference will happen at eight a.m.,' he said, even though they both knew when it was. He would have said almost anything to break the silence between them.

She nodded.

'Then we will travel back to Farrehed for the state funeral.'

She nodded again.

'I'll be incredibly busy over the next few months, and I want you to know that it's not because of you. It is because of what my country needs.'

'I understand.'

Her quiet acceptance only frustrated him more. Especially as it was delivered in such a way that made it sound as if he were delivering a punishment rather than an order of events.

'When all this settles down I promise you we will find a way to bring your friend to Farrehed and we will find peace…between us.'

'I understand,' she repeated, still looking out of the window at the streets of London as they twisted and turned down the roads that would lead them to the embassy.

Something like panic gripped him—concern that maybe she wasn't well.

'Are you okay?'

'Yes, perfectly.'

'You must be tired. You've been awake since seven a.m. yesterday.'

'Has it been that long?'

The detached tone of her voice, so very different from the sounds made by the woman who had cried his name only two hours before, pierced him somewhere within his chest.

'Time waits for no woman,' she said, turning to him with a small smile. 'Not even a queen.'

Odir released his hold on the overhead handrail before he broke it. He considered kissing her again. He was desperate to do something—anything—to bring back the heat, the fire that had been there earlier that evening.

It had reminded him of when he had first met Eloise. She'd been so full of light... But on reflection he could see now that that light had been reserved for the times when her father hadn't been there.

Odir had taken her acceptance of his proposal for granted—as a side effect of their fathers' close relationship. He'd somehow managed to convince himself it was what she wanted. But now, in his mind, he ran over their conversations during their engagement—what he'd taken for shared confidences—and saw only polite exchanges, not really digging deeper into the woman he had desired with a need that had almost undone him, undone his country.

He'd told himself his absence from her was due to the fact that he hadn't had any time, and he'd clung to that in desperation—because if it wasn't that, then it was because he had been hiding from his wife. That he had been a coward. Too much of a coward to take what he'd wanted...what he'd felt simmering beneath the surface of their every interaction.

Looking back on endless nights spent in the furthest reaches of the palace, separated from her by empty rooms and duty, he knew his wife had become a source of impossible temptation and censure.

In public she was perfect. Poised, but sensitive. Kind and caring, but regal. In private she had become an ache, a thorn in his side—one that now whispered across the months of time, *Why don't you want me?* The thought pierced his deepest secrets, sounding so very much like himself as a child, looking to his father, wanting to know why he wasn't enough to spare the man pain.

And suddenly every action, every sacrifice Eloise had made during their brief marriage, became overlaid by his own attempts to reach out to a man too distant, too emotionally shut off to love him.

An arrow of pain sliced through Odir and he wondered whether he had made a sound—because Eloise's eyes were suddenly on him and full of concern. His heart started to pound beneath his chest, and in his mind, just for a second, he wanted to call it all off. He wanted to send her away from the questions and needs that he wasn't sure he could answer.

The limousine turned left and pulled to a stop before wrought-iron gates. A small crowd had begun to gather in front of the embassy, backed by several news trucks. Figures huddled in the dark, sipping from plastic cups with wisps of steam curling into the night air, throwing cigarette ends into the street away from the pavement, their badges flashing into the night proclaiming them world-renowned news crews.

Before they could move through the gates a couple of flashbulbs burst through the tinted windows, highlighting Eloise's drawn features. But the quiet growl of the powerful engine beneath them glided them forward through the iron gates and into the embassy courtyard.

Men dressed in black flanked the side entrance to the building, two moving to open the doors to the town car, and Odir regretted it. Some ancient sense of inbuilt propriety had him wanting to open Eloise's door himself and lead her out into the night air.

Eloise's heeled feet nearly slipped on the cobbles, and she clung to Malik's arm like a lifeline. She took a deep breath and steeled herself. This was her life now. It had been once before, but now...now she knew her reasons for being there.

She forced a smile, turning her head to where the cameras eagerly sought their mark, and gave a small wave. Not too happy—it would not be the done thing to appear happy with the news that they were about to share with the world's media. Calls for her to smile, questions about where she had been, demands to know if the rumours about her pregnancy were real—a thousand voices swirled around her with one word ringing in her ears. *Baby, baby, baby*.

For a second her smile faltered, just as Malik positioned his body between her and the media behind them. *A baby*. They had twice had unprotected sex tonight. She had come to the party seeking a divorce and left the party possibly pregnant, definitely still married and about to become a queen.

Her hand went reflexively to her abdomen. Could she bring a child into the world with parents who... who...?

Could she still claim that she did not love Odir? She might be willing to fool the world's media, but after all this time she was done with fooling herself.

They might have only slept together for the first time that evening, but she had known this man for two years. She knew how he took his coffee, she knew that he hated to swim, she knew that he felt more at home on horseback than in any powerful car, and she knew that he would sacrifice anything for the protection of his people—even his own heart.

She knew the sound he made when he found his completion within her—had felt it echo within her breast. And she knew that within her heart of hearts, buried deep within its recesses, beneath all the secrets and lies that had built up between them, she had always loved her husband.

'Your Majesty?' Malik prompted softly.

The clipped sound of her heels on the cobblestones cut through her thoughts as Malik led her to where Odir was waiting halfway up the steps and then towards a non-descript side door, partially opened on the inviting light and warmth of the embassy before her.

Odir's security detail, having received word that the press had surrounded the front steps of the Embassy, had decided to use the side entrance and led them through sleek industrial kitchens, where staff were already beginning to prep for the day. Each and every one of them stopped what they were doing and bowed their heads with a respect that settled peace within Eloise's heart. She was a part of this, helping to create happiness not only for these people but for an entire country that very much needed healing. And she allowed that knowledge to warm her. To give her strength.

From the kitchens they were led into a hallway, and then they covered the distance to the central state room at a fast pace. Hearing the hushed tones and feeling the silent respect of every single person they passed, Eloise felt the weight of that responsibility. She looked to her husband, at the broad shoulders ready and willing to take as much of it as was needed. But his back appeared frozen with a tension she had not seen before. His left shoulder was just a centimetre higher than the other—the only outward indication that he wasn't as relaxed as he appeared.

And suddenly Eloise understood the difference between the previous signs of respect she had witnessed Odir encountering and those she saw now. The bows were just that little bit deeper, the smiles on the faces of his staff more sincere, and tinged with so much more than respect.

They knew.

They knew that his father was dead and that they were now standing before the Sheikh who would take them back from the brink of civil war and bring them to a new era of peace and prosperity.

Eloise felt rather than saw Odir's step falter, so attuned to his body now, in a way that she had never been before. And she knew that he had realised, almost at the same time, the reason for the heavy silence about them. A combination of grief and hope.

His powerful stride took them from the rich red hues of the state room and out into the warm gold and white of the central hallway. Eloise took in impressions of colour, rather than specific details, for her eyes only had one goal. Her husband.

In the main foyer, beneath a large, expansive white marble staircase, there were even more people. Men in suits instead of kitchen whites hurried between the rooms off the foyer, papers and tablets in hand, calling for corrections to statements and prepared interviews, demanding changes to itineraries planned for months ahead.

All of them came to a sudden halt on seeing Odir.

Only one figure had been still and silent, watching their approach with hooded eyes. Eyes that sought Eloise rather than Odir.

Jarhan might have fooled those about him with his relaxed stance, but Eloise recognised it for what it was. A façade. And when their gazes met she could read the fear written there. The fear that her return to his brother's side meant that his secret was out.

Odir caught sight of his brother at the same instant Eloise did. Of all the people in the room, the only one not looking at him was Jarhan. He felt the familiar instinctual reaction rise within him— fury, anger, jealousy, and one word that echoed in his brain—*mine!*

And then he came to a crashing halt. It wasn't lust painted in his brother's eyes. It wasn't desire or need, but *fear*. This was the brother he'd tried to protect as a young child—protect from his father's grief, from his own. The brother he'd taught to ride, made toys with, conjured up imaginary castles and battles, commanded rebellions and cut down tin soldiers... The brother who had been forced to live a lie, forced to hide his own sexuality, forced to sacrifice his own happiness. The brother who had been innocent of all accusations...

Again he wondered how he'd never seen it.

Jarhan wasn't effeminate—he was almost as strong and commanding as himself. But he would still be castigated for his feelings, for his desires. His father would have exiled him—would have cut him from their family, never allowing his name to be uttered within the palace walls.

But Odir was not his father.

Amongst a sea of bowed heads only three remained upright, and finally Jarhan met his gaze. And instead of anger or recrimination—the two things that had tainted their every interaction in the last six months—Odir felt...*love*.

Shockingly powerful and utterly protective, the feeling nearly knocked Odir off his feet.

He crossed the expanse of the foyer between them in five long strides and took his brother in his arms in an embrace that he hoped would convey even just an ounce of what he was feeling. Grief, love, loss, pain and regret all swirled within him. And it felt... *good*. Good to embrace all these feelings without secrets and lies, without shame and anger.

His brother's body—at first held as stiff as the tin soldiers they had once played with—relaxed into his hold, and Odir felt wet heat press against his closed eyes. Jarhan stirred and tried to say something. But Odir cut him off.

'Can you ever forgive me?' Odir whispered into his brother's ear.

'Can you forgive *me*?'

'Already done, Jar.' Using the childhood nickname brought a broken smile to his brother's features. 'Already done.'

There would be a time for words. That time would be soon, but it wasn't now.

'You'll fly back with us after the press conference and we'll talk. We'll talk properly.'

'Us?' Jarhan queried.

Odir glanced over to Eloise who, unlike the two

men, had failed to prevent the tears in her eyes from finding a trail down her cheeks. She brushed them aside and the smile that almost reached her eyes poked at the sensitive heart learning to beat again beneath his chest.

'You will be by our side at the press conference.'

'I'm not sure—'

'I *am*,' he interrupted.

He would begin his rule properly—united with his brother and his wife—no matter what might come in the future. Odir *wanted* this. Not for his country, not for his people, but for himself. And by God he would make it happen.

Jarhan left them to get ready for the press conference and Odir dismissed his guards. He directed Eloise to the central staircase at the back of the embassy that led to the private suites on the fourth floor. This was the lowest building in the possession of the Farrehed royal family, and in comparison to Heron Tower it was almost laughable, but he had always liked this embassy.

It wasn't a palace, but he and Jarhan had looked forward to holidays here as children. Odir's feet carved a pathway over the rich burgundy carpet that had intricate patterns he could still strangely remember from his childhood.

Somewhere in the distance of his memory he heard the laughter of children disappearing around one of the corners of the embassy, followed by his mother's light call for both her children. He would never hear the sound of her voice again, nor that of his father's. Both his parents were gone.

He wasn't fool enough to think that he didn't need to grieve. He was a prince—a king—not a madman. He just couldn't allow himself the time—not yet. Maybe not even for some months.

Eloise shifted beside him, drawing him out of his thoughts and eyeing him with something suspiciously like compassion. He wondered how it was that she seemed to see right through him to his deepest thoughts. This woman he had not even seen in six months, to whom he had not made love until tonight—a woman who might be pregnant with his child.

For a moment it all felt too much. His father, Eloise, *her* father, his brother... It was all swirling around in his exhausted mind.

He felt Eloise take the card that had been given to him by Malik and saw her type the passcode written on the back into the electronic pad beside the door. She turned to him and smiled and the breath left his lungs—she looked...naughty, cheeky, impish. Not a look he remembered seeing.

'I feel like I'm in a spy film.'

'Well, I *do* know how to kill someone with my little finger,' he replied, the response rolling off his tongue before he could censor it.

Her laughter was glorious. Uninhibited. And it was something that he wanted to hear again.

She pushed open the door and continued talking to him over her shoulder. There was something incredibly and oddly domestic about it, and he couldn't tell if he'd walked into a dream or a nightmare.

'It was good what you did with Jarhan,' she said, disappearing into the room.

'Good?'

'Yes—kind.'

'Kindness has nothing to do with it. He's my brother.'

'Mmm…'

'What's that supposed to mean?'

'Nothing… Well, I was just wondering what you would have done had he not been gay and had actually *meant* it when he kissed me.'

She turned, casting those blue eyes on him once again, and he couldn't tell whether she was serious or not.

'I would have married him off to his first cousin once removed.'

'A terrible fate, I'm sure.'

Another smile lifted those lips and he felt as if the sun had burst through the clouds.

'You haven't met her!'

'So you have a sense of humour, Your Majesty?'

'Shh, don't tell anyone.'

A shadow passed across her features. 'I remember it. From before our wedding. You would wield it like a sword, cutting through the tension and making me laugh.'

He remembered it too.

'I used to think…' She trailed off, as if unsure she should continue.

He held her gaze, held his breath, ridiculously desperate to hear what she'd used to think.

'I used to think that you were my Prince Charming,' she said, collapsing into a plush chair in the living room. She looked almost dainty, nestled within the cushions. 'That you would come and rescue me from my evil father.'

'I still can, Eloise.'

'Surely in this day and age a princess should be able to rescue herself, no?' she asked, and he heard a thread of uncertainty enter her voice, slowly withering him from the inside.

'You tried that, *habibti*.'

'And you found me.'

He took a deep breath. 'I wouldn't have. Not without Malik. I still think he only told me because of my father's death.' She looked down at her hands. 'How did you do it?'

'Do what?'

'Manage to convince one of the most loyal men I know to betray me.'

A sad smile covered her features. Almost conciliatory. As if she knew how much that betrayal had hurt. 'Would it help if I said it wasn't about you?'

'That man's whole *life* has been about me.'

She sighed. 'He knew about Jarhan.'

'Sweet Lord—am I the only one who didn't?'

'No,' she said lightly, almost affectionately. 'No. But Malik knew because the protection detail knew. It was part of Jarhan's main concern. That he might give Farrehed's enemies a weakness in your rule.'

'But that is not why Malik obtained the passport, Eloise.'

'No… He followed me after you had told me to leave. Found me. It must have been quite a shock for him. I was throwing things into a suitcase and my father was on speaker phone. I was asking to come home, but he wouldn't allow it. Said that if I set foot in England he would have my mother transferred to a clinic—that he would bury her under the weight of the world's press. Ensure that I never saw her again.'

Odir heard the tremor in her voice and could only imagine what her fear must have been like then, on that night.

'I've… I've never felt more helpless in my life, Odir. There I was—a princess, wife of a sheikh soon to be a ruler of nations—and I couldn't do anything. I couldn't come to you. I couldn't go home. Malik cut the phone call, sat me down and made me tell him everything. For five hours we talked about different options and came up with a plan. I asked him. I asked him why he was willing to help me.'

'Did he tell you?' Odir asked.

He very much doubted that Malik would have

revealed how close to the bone Eloise's story would have cut him. The only people who knew about Malik's past were Malik, his family, and Odir.

'All he said was that so long as he knew where I was, what name I was under, then he would help. Now I see that the person he was helping was you.'

Eloise knew that she should feel hurt by that realisation. But she didn't. She was pleased that there was someone who looked out for her husband. The husband who was surrounded by hundreds of people, all ready to serve and protect him, but none to care for him. None to put him first.

His mother's death had left him adrift, in the hands of a father so cut down by grief he had been jealous of his son's power. He had mistrusted and distanced himself from the first person he should have been caring for. And, God, did she know how much *that* hurt.

But she did care for her husband. She felt the knowledge settle within her, warm her, spreading throughout her body and mind like wildfire, energising her thoughts and actions.

Restless, she got up from the chair and walked through the suite, curious as to its layout and its luxury, until she found herself in an elaborate bedroom, designed with the same glory as the rest of the embassy.

The sight of the large, modern, sleek bed reminded Eloise of Odir's promise earlier that evening, and in an instant her body was ready. She ran her fingers over lips that still felt bruised from their earlier kisses, wanting to cover her mouth, to stop the words that were filling her heart from falling from her lips. Otherwise they'd escape, and they'd speak of her feelings for him, of this new, delicate love she had found.

She knew he wasn't ready to hear those words from her. Not yet. But perhaps she could show him. With her touches...with her kisses.

The ripple of desire lifted the hairs on her arms. Her body was throbbing between legs which she drew together to clamp down on the wet heat of need. How had she become so cravenly wanton in just a matter of hours?

Odir loomed behind her and the air about them which had so recently been full of confession was suddenly thick with desire. Eloise inhaled it deeply, wanting it to fill her, needing it. Her body moved of its own volition, pressing back against the hard planes of her husband's chest. Someone groaned—whether it was her or him Eloise couldn't tell any more.

His lips came down upon her bare shoulder and his arms wrapped around her breast and lower stomach. He gathered the silk of her gown in his hand, bunching it against the top of her thigh, whilst his fingers played with her nipple already hard beneath his touch.

'I keep my promises, *habibti*,' he whispered wickedly in her ear.

She heard the desperation that quivered in his words…rejoiced in the fact that he was as quickly undone as she. Her arms reached behind her, bringing him and his arousal closer against her body. The action reminded her of earlier that evening, when they had been beneath the night sky. And this time she knew it was *she* who groaned, the sensuality of the sound shocking herself.

'When you make that noise it drives me wild, Eloise. Look what you do to me,' he said, turning her in his arms to face him. *'Look.'*

The guttural tone of his words ran through her. She *did* see what she did to him. And she wanted to show him what he did to her. How he made her feel. What he'd given back to her in these last hours. The undoing of the past. She wanted to show him how it could be. What their marriage could be like.

He took her hand and pressed it against the length of his powerful arousal. Hard, hot and utterly the most magnificent thing she had ever felt. To have this man—this ruler of a kingdom—at her command was inconceivable. And she wanted it more than she wanted her next breath.

His mouth came down on hers and she relished it. Relished the power that burned between them now that they had been stripped bare of all the lies and secrets. Each time they had come together it had been to use this passion, this insatiable need, in order to escape. But she wasn't hiding any more. All of her was open to him, exposed to him in a way she hadn't been before.

And it was shocking in its intensity.

If she had thought coming together with him before had been incredible, it was nothing in comparison to this. She clung to every second, every touch, every taste, revelling in the energy that brought her alive within his embrace.

As his tongue pressed into her mouth she took it, long and deep, within her. She fought to match him, plunged her own tongue into the wet heat of his. Instead of bringing capitulation it enflamed their mutual desire. Teeth scraped against tongues, lips grazed against teeth, and heart clashed against heart.

His hands came down around her backside and lifted her against him. Her shoes dropped onto the floor as he marched them over to the bed. Instead of letting her go he stood there, holding her in his arms, allowing her open legs to press against his erection, and she shifted her hips forward to feel the tip of his arousal meet her core.

She rocked her hips once more and it was enough.

He knelt on the bed and laid her down, maintaining a kiss that served only to bring them closer. He kicked off his shoes, tore at his shirt, and as she

lifted her dress over her head he rid himself of his
trousers and underwear.

He stood over her, naked and glorious. 'I need
you, Eloise,' he said, his voice grave and thick with
passion.

She nodded, but it wasn't enough. Odir needed to
hear her say it too. The extent of that need scared
him, but now was not a time for fear.

He spread her beautiful legs, opening her to him.
'Say it.'

He saw her struggle to find the words and something primal rose within him. Primal and demanding.

'Say it.'

He watched as the look in her eyes transformed
into something fierce—a recognition of what he
needed and what she so desperately wanted. She was
utterly glorious, naked and perfect. Her breasts rose
in time with her short breaths and Odir knew that he
was standing on a precipice—that it was more than
desire burning between them.

'I need you too.'

He sank into her warm, wet heat, pressing as far
as he could possibly reach, and there—up to the
hilt—he finally found what he had been looking for.

But somehow it still wasn't enough.

She was wrapped around his length, and he felt
sensation upon sensation as she raised her hips to
take him even further. His curses littered the air

about them as he lifted her leg from the bed and placed it over his shoulder, finding an even deeper purchase. Her impassioned gasp teased him, and he silently promised them both that he would make this marriage *more*. More than it had been.

He withdrew so slowly, so exquisitely, and despite his intention of driving her wild with need he nearly came. He withdrew completely and then returned to her, so deeply inside her that he felt entwined with her—more than him and more than her, something new and bigger than each of them alone.

How could one person feel all these things? Eloise wondered.

The need within her was rising to an unfamiliar height as again he withdrew from her, but this time she wasn't going to let him have his way. She reached behind him and drew him back into her. But the illusion of power was simply that—an illusion. He had *let* her have control and she thanked him for it. She pulled him against her, pressing him deeper within her, and smiled when he accused her of trying to kill him.

Her husband had given her the freedom to vent her wildest fantasies, and whilst she might not have experience her body knew what it desired, what it needed. He must have read it in her expression, seen it in her eyes, because right there, buried deep within her, he gathered her in his arms and rolled onto his back.

Eloise shifted her legs, her knees either side of his thighs, and almost cried out loud. Never before had she experienced this kind of completeness or felt so connected to another person.

She rocked forwards and backwards and knew from the words that exploded from Odir's mouth that he was as close as she was to orgasm. She savoured this moment…the power that she had to give them what they both so desperately wanted. She felt powerful in all the ways she once had not.

But soon all thought was driven from her mind as cries of pleasure fell from her lips, drowned in the sound of Odir's ragged breath, and she was launched into a world of starlight and sensation as the two of them found their completion.

CHAPTER ELEVEN

August 2nd, 06.00-07.00, Farrehed Embassy

FOR A MOMENT Eloise thought it might have been the sound of the shower that had pulled her from her dreamless sleep. For a second she was confused. She looked about the room, but knew she wasn't in Heron Tower any more. Then it came again. A pounding on the door. The kind of urgent pounding that refused to be ignored.

Odir flung the door of the bathroom back on its hinges and she could almost believe that it had left a dent in the wall.

'What?' he barked from the bedroom, his voice clearly travelling far enough to reach the intruder out in the hall.

Eloise shook her head, trying to dislodge the webs of sleep that had wrapped themselves around her mind. She looked at the clock and could scarcely believe that she'd been asleep for only twenty minutes. She felt as if she'd slept for a year.

She could hear hushed voices through the wall, and knew that the world was about to intrude.

And what would they find? A naked, soon-to-be queen lying in her husband's bed! She bit back a smile that wouldn't quit from the way that Odir had made her feel...protected, safe...*loved*.

And that was what it was. The excitement thrumming through her veins. The thought that after all this time, all the secrets, all the truths of that night, it was possible to fall in love in only ten hours.

But it wasn't just ten hours. She had known Odir for two years. She had watched him bear the weight of his country, watched him care for his brother, struggle with his father, confront the past and transform into an intensely passionate lover.

Any lingering tiredness she felt was pushed away with the tingling buzz of optimism and hope. After all this time could she actually find happiness with Odir? Could she find someone who would *love* her?

Next door, the tenor of the conversation had changed, and with a small squeak she leapt out of bed and hurried through to the bathroom, closing the door behind her and trapping herself in the heat and steam of Odir's recent shower.

She wiped the mist that had gathered over the large mirror. Her reflection showed a woman truly ravished, bright-eyed and admittedly looking a little crazy. She took a deep breath. It would be fine. They would find a way to make it through the next few hours, and then the next few days. They would make it work.

Her mother was seeking support for her addiction, Natalia would also have the help she needed. Farrehed would have the ruler it deserved and she would have the husband she had always wanted. It was possible—and it was all within her reach.

She gave her reflection a small victorious smile and then stepped beneath the hot spray of the shower.

'It is impossible. I cannot do it,' Odir said, trying to keep the fury from his voice. Even in front of his aide he must keep his controlled façade.

He thought back to minutes earlier, when he had let it slip. For his wife, and—God help him—for himself.

'My King, they need this reassurance.'

'I appreciate that, Lamir, but it is not going to happen. My first priority upon returning to Farrehed will be to address my people. Not to meet the ruler of Kalaran. Our allies will have time with me, but it won't be until after the funeral.'

'But—'

'There *are* no buts.'

Odir looked around the suite that had been blissfully empty only moments before. Now he felt as if he had been invaded by soldiers—suited and booted individuals armed with laptops, stacks of paper and pens, shooting demands at him left, right and centre.

Another aide thrust a piece of paper into his hand and he marvelled at how he was supposed to feel regal and all-powerful when he seemed to be at the mercy of his staff. The document was the approval for the opening of talks with Farrehed's desert tribal leaders in an attempt to begin the healing process.

Why did he feel as if he'd just ripped open a wound? All night he'd felt driven to the point in time when, in one hour, he would announce his father's death. All night he'd ensured that what needed to be done had been done. That all the players who were needed were in place.

He'd felt capable, driven, motivated. And yet suddenly now he was feeling helpless, unsure, a little bit lost. And it had nothing to do with the chaos surrounding him. It was to do with the woman one room away, standing in the centre of the storm with him.

It was already beginning. He should be focusing on all the things that must be done, but he was completely distracted by his wife.

'Sir, I need you to sign the release form on the press briefing.'

'I appreciate that...' He searched for the bespectacled kid's name—the man couldn't be more than twenty-two—but it eluded him. 'But I'm sure that you wouldn't want news to get out that the first official communication dealt with by the new Sheikh of Farrehed was approved when he was wearing a dressing gown and nothing else.'

He was sure that it was only a will almost as strong as his own that prevented the fresh-faced aide from casting him a full-length appraisal.

'Five minutes.'

'But, Sir—'

In lieu of a response Odir glared at the boy for a full ten seconds before he left the room.

Odir could do nothing to prevent the curse falling from his lips as he slammed the bedroom door behind him, startling Eloise as she came out of the bathroom wrapped in nothing but a fluffy white towel.

'We have company,' he said, in response to her raised eyebrow.

'So I gathered.'

'And by "company" I mean about twenty people crammed into what should be considered a luxurious and sizeable living room. They seem to be going to war using technology and documents.'

'We'll handle it,' she said.

There was something different about her. Something he didn't want to question. He *knew* they would handle it. They had to.

'I have to get dressed.'

'That's a shame,' she replied.

And, again, he couldn't quite fathom the almost flirtatious nature of her tone.

'Shame or not, it has to be done. Hair and Make-Up need the room.'

'You're having your hair and make-up done?'

'No, Eloise, *you* are.'

'Oh.'

He regretted his words the instant that warm smile disappeared from her features.

He went to the wardrobe and pulled out the suit that had been waiting for him there since yesterday afternoon. Right next to the hanger that contained her dress. It had been hastily vetted by the PR team and now he wondered whether it might be a bit loose, considering the weight Eloise had lost in the last few months.

He ruthlessly pushed that thought from his mind. Right now he needed to focus on what was going on next door.

He stepped into his boxers and pulled on the suit trousers, aware that Eloise's eyes never once left his body. He felt a strange heat enter his bones, lying thick in his veins, and forced back the desire that began to throb within him.

'I won't…' He struggled to find words, strangely tongue-tied before his wife. 'I won't have much time for you today. After the press conference we'll be moving to the airfield from where we'll fly to Farrehed.'

If anything could cut through the fog of desire building between them, Eloise thought, *that* was it.

She knew it was time to put on the mask. That she

would wear the dress that she had noticed hanging in the wardrobe next to the suit her husband would be wearing. A dress that had been picked out for her most probably before she'd even left Zurich.

But where once she had thought that this was the part she hated, Eloise now steeled herself. She wanted to be there, standing beside her husband when he made his announcement to the world's press. Wanted to support him in this. So she would wear that dress the same way she would continue to wear his ring. As his bride and as his Queen.

She walked over to the closet and took out the dress covered by a protective zipped bag. Hanging on the same hanger was underwear and hosiery, and she felt a flush of embarrassment knowing that it hadn't been Odir who had picked them out for her in a passion-fuelled desire to see her in them. It would have been some faceless member of staff—possibly someone sitting now on the other side of that door—who had picked out suitable clothes for Odir's press conference.

The dress would have been weighed up, possibly even polled, to see what people's reactions would be. It wouldn't be overtly sexy. It would probably cover her arms to her wrists, with no hint of cleavage, but nor would she look like a prim Victorian matron.

The irony wasn't lost on her. She couldn't look too appealing, but nor could she look cold and aloof. It would be the Goldilocks of dresses and she would have to be the Goldilocks of queens.

'I'll get changed in the bathroom.'

'I'll be next door when you come out. Should I tell Hair and Make-Up—?'

'Send them in. I'll not be long.'

'Eloise—'

Her name sounded strange on his tongue this time, almost regretful, and the sound tugged on her heart and turned her around.

'It's okay. I understand.'

She couldn't work out why that didn't seem to settle him. She smiled before stepping into the bathroom with the dress, hoping that might reassure him. Reassure them both, even.

In the bathroom, she slipped the towel from around her and let it fall to the floor. Oddly, it felt as if she had lost some form of protection. As if the barrier between her and the world outside was gone.

She unwrapped the brand-new underwear from its cellophane. It felt expensive and new against her skin.

She slid the zip down on the cover of the dress without looking beneath it. With her eyes on anything else in the bathroom, she pulled the dress from its hanger and stood holding it limply in her hands.

This was the moment when her life would change. No matter the decisions and the promises from earlier that evening, Eloise knew that the moment she put on this dress was the moment that she would be irrevocably his.

When she emerged Eloise thought she'd stepped into an alternative reality. When only moments before it had only been Odir in the room, now there were four people—none of whom she recognised from her life at the palace before.

She frowned. 'Where is Victoria?' she asked, wondering why the woman who had been her royal stylist from six months before their wedding wasn't there.

A small blonde woman turned and in clipped, professional tones delivered the news that Victoria was back in Farrehed, having given birth two weeks earlier.

Life goes on, Eloise realised. First Anders and now Victoria.

For all the time she had been in Zurich, going to work, spending precious time with Natalia, watching the seasons change in that beautiful city, learning that she liked helping to organise her boss's day and hating the loneliness of the nights, Eloise had never imagined time continuing in Farrehed. But it wasn't a magical kingdom that had slept in her absence. It was a soon-to-be thriving country under Odir's care and rule.

The small blonde who was still yet to introduce

herself gestured for her to take a seat at the bedroom's opulent dressing table. Eloise padded over
to the chair, her feet separated from the plush carpet
by the silk stockings covering her legs, numbing her
from the touch of the mundane or the real.

'We had to guess at your size, Your Majesty.' The
line was delivered without reproach or curiosity. 'We
chose black, as the situation demands, but allowed
for the lines of the dress to highlight your femininity.
It would not be done to have you looking all *boxy*.'

The woman sniffed, as if such a thing would be the
greatest offence. It grated on Eloise's fragile nerves.

'It is the perfect dress for the occasion,' she
found herself responding, and it must have been the
right thing to say for the woman seemed eminently
pleased.

'There are changes of clothes ready on the jet
that will take you to Farrehed. These will be in the
traditional style, and will match the King's as he
makes his first appearance to the public after the
announcement.'

Eloise tuned out the soft litany falling from the
woman's lips as she pulled and pushed the dress
about her frame to ensure that it was fitting correctly. A man bobbed up and down behind her, teasing tangles out of her hair with a brush, whilst at the
same time another girl started applying make-up as
if she were an artist with oils and paintbrushes rather
than concealer and mascara.

When someone dipped behind her in front of the hairstylist and looped a string of pearls around her neck Eloise tried her hardest not to flinch. They were the same style of pearls that her mother had worn when Eloise was a child. Her hand hovered just beneath the pearls, as if reluctant to touch them—fearful, even. Eloise had never worn pearls for that very reason, and in her mind she was flung back almost twenty years.

She'd been hiding in her favourite place—the bottom of her mother's wardrobe. It had been dark and warm, her body surrounded by silk and velvet and the finest cotton, and there had been just enough space in the gap between the doors to watch her mother as she prepared herself for another function. Cream. Her mother always wore cream.

She would sit at her dressing table, surrounded by make-up, perfume, and the most beautiful jewellery. It was all so very grown-up, and as a child Eloise had wanted it so badly.

As her mother had applied the base for her make-up, blusher and eye shadow, little Eloise had copied her every movement, swirling an imaginary brush in the palm of her hand, smoothing it over soft cheeks still plump with childhood.

The haze of a child's imagination had coloured in the spaces with fairy tales of magical evenings full of dancing and serenity, believing the emotion glittering in her mother's eyes was excitement rather than what Eloise could see it for now…sadness and the effect of prescription medication.

Curled up in the corner of the wardrobe, her knees clutched to her chest, every time she had thought that *this* would be the time her mother would notice her hiding place. That this would be the time her mother would find her and kiss her goodnight, tell her that she loved her.

Every time until that last time. When through the reflection in the mirror they had locked eyes, and all the hope of her mother finally coming to kiss her goodnight had disappeared when the only thing her mother had offered her was a small smile before leaving the room.

Eloise had never hidden in her mother's wardrobe again.

Her mother had not loved her. Not in the way that she had needed as a child. She couldn't hold that against her—Angelina simply wasn't capable of it. Even now. But Eloise was different. She *was* capable of love—she knew that now. She deserved love. She deserved someone who would put her before the parties, before the social engagements, before anything and anyone else.

The tug of her wedding ring being taken from her finger brought her back to the present with a shock, and she instinctively closed her hand in a fist.

'What do you think you are doing?' she demanded.

'As I said, Your Majesty, we need to place a snuggy inside your ring.'

'A *snuggy*?' She realised her voice was high and loud but didn't care.

'Yes, ma'am. Your ring—it's loose. This is a piece of plastic that will sit inside the ring to make it tighter around your finger, so that it won't slip during the press conference.'

Even though the man sounded apologetic she didn't care. He was holding up a ridiculously small, horribly grey plastic band as if it were the most important thing in the world. As if somehow it would make her wedding ring fit. As if it would cover the tiny gap between her being royal and her *not* being royal. Her being Odir's wife and *not* being Odir's wife.

Someone entered the bedroom behind her, and in the reflection of the mirror, through the open door, her eyes found her husband's. All night she had felt the weight of her husband's gaze and the power held there, whether it was in sexual attraction, arrogance or anger. But in that moment she clung to it desperately, as if they were two people in the eye of a storm not of their own making.

She made herself look away. She felt numb—or she felt too much. She couldn't quite work which. It was as if she couldn't feel any of it. Even the weight of the wedding ring as it was pushed back tightly onto her finger.

Suddenly she was that little girl again, hiding in the corner of the closet, waiting for someone to find her. Waiting for someone to love her.

And she couldn't do it.

She couldn't be that scared little girl any more.

'Clear the room.'

Odir's command stopped everyone in their tracks. Startled faces looked back at him. All but Eloise's. The stylist looked as if she might disagree, but Odir had stared down armies of men, and he watched as the woman realised as much. All four people hastily scrambled from the room and disappeared through the door.

His wife had still not looked at him.

He prowled over to the chair. He knew that he towered over her, but he couldn't help it. His wife looked incredible, but she also looked untouchable and he didn't like it.

Her fingers reached up behind her neck and struggled with a string of pearls that didn't suit her at all. There was something in the way that she fought with the necklace that sent a shiver of fear through him.

'I think it's caught in my—'

He brushed her fingers aside and undid the clasp. He smoothed away the few errant strands of hair that had become caught in the clasp and the moment the necklace was secured he felt peace settle around him.

'You look magnificent,' he said, settling his hands on her slim shoulders.

She was *here*. Beneath his fingers and his touch. And she would be standing beside him in an hour, when he made his announcement to the press. They would talk on the plane. They would figure it all out. He'd take her to bed and take away the fear he could see in her eyes.

'Odir—'

He knew what she wanted, but in that moment he would do anything to make her stop.

'Odir, I—'

'Don't say it. For the love of God, don't say it, Eloise.'

'I have to.'

'No, you don't.'

'Yes, I do. I will *not* be like my mother. I will *not* be anything like either of my parents, Odir. I cannot live my life afraid to say the one thing that fills me so completely. I love you.'

Somewhere deep within him something broke loose. Fear and fury took over his body and his mind.

He felt his lips draw into a grim line. 'No, you don't,' he growled. It was a warning more than a denial.

'It's not something that you can command or control. It's not something you can order removed from your life. It's mine—mine to give.'

'I refuse to accept it.'

'What? My love or the fact that you can't control it?'

He couldn't answer that question even if he'd wanted to.

'Through everything you've tried to do,' she continued—her words beating against his heart, smashing through the walls that he'd carefully placed around it to protect himself. '*Everything*, Odir—bribery, blackmail, lies and cheating—through it all it's still here. I still feel it for you.'

'Love is weakness, Eloise,' he barked, as if he could convince her of it too. 'Love destroys. Look at your mother. A woman who would seek oblivion and secrecy over her daughter's happiness! How good is love then? And my father! Look at him. If I am to be any kind of ruler—any kind that is far from the destruction my father caused because of his love—then love will never be part of my life.'

He knew that he was shouting now. Knew that he'd lost the control he'd so desperately clung to all evening. Lost the one thing that had got him through the day and the night.

'You ask what kind of ruler you will be… You have spent so long looking to the future, Odir, that you don't realise you have already *been* the kind of ruler to protect your country for the last few years. You have done more for Farrehed in those years than your father ever did to drag it backwards in *thirty*. You have faced rebellion and smoothed it over. You have faced negligence and done everything in your power to counter it. You have created programmes to ensure the protection of disadvantaged and desperate people who will thrive in years to come.'

Her breath was now as ragged as his own. But there was power in her words. It was as if she were conjuring up a battle cry, and yet he only had an inkling of what that battle would be.

'You have the love of your people, and even if you don't believe in the power of that love, the strength of that love, they *do* love you. And so do I.'

He knew they were on the brink of something. He could see them both on the edge of a crack in the centre of the earth. She was stepping back from him. And no matter how much he reached for her she was withdrawing from him, eluding his grasp.

'You said yes, Eloise.' His voice was raw and low. 'You said you'd come back. Be by my side. You can't take that back. You can't leave now.'

The look in her eyes cut him to the core. It was sadness and pity. It was so different from the way she had looked at him earlier in the evening, when she had believed he could hang the moon wherever she wanted. Could protect her from all her demons. Now she was looking at him as if *he* were the demon. As if he could hurt her more than all her experiences combined.

'You don't need me—and deep down I think you know it.'

No. In his mind he denied it. And deep within his chest his heart was beating hard enough to be heard.

'All this talk of love, Eloise, is nothing but an excuse. An excuse for you to run away.'

She shook her head in fierce denial. 'It's not, Odir. I am not running. I'm standing and fighting. But I won't come back as your wife, no matter the threats or the bribes, unless you *do* love me.'

'What you want is impossible.' His arm slashed through the air before him, as if trying to cut her down. 'I'm not even sure that I'm capable of it.'

Only for the first time he realised that he was lying to himself. He knew that what she was saying was true. He *could* rule without her. He'd done it for the last six months. He didn't need her by his side to make the announcement, and he didn't need her by his side to rule. Because he *did* love his people. And she was right—that *did* make him powerful and strong.

All evening he'd managed to lie to himself and convince himself that he needed her by his side. But if he was brutally honest it had nothing to do with ruling, or with Farrehed. He'd wanted her back because he'd never been able to get her out of his mind. Because he'd never been able to forget the young woman who had once captured his heart with her laugh.

What she'd achieved in the name of love—marrying him in order to protect her mother, turning her back on wealth and power and still being able to protect her friend—the transformation she had undergone, the independence she had thrived under for the last six months… And in just two hours he'd seen the damage he'd caused to that new fire within her. He'd seen her retreat behind a façade, and that had hurt him more than he could ever have imagined.

Because he *did* love her.

Everything in him rose up with love and the need to protect her.

He *did* love this incredible woman.

But his position as King, as ruler of his country, would mean that he couldn't offer her the life she deserved, the *love* she deserved. He couldn't keep her behind that façade she put on to combat the difficulty of life in the public eye.

Back in the limo, on their way to the embassy, the fire in her, the light, had been extinguished. He couldn't tie her to a life of duty. He couldn't—no, *wouldn't*—make her live a life of sacrifice for a country that wasn't even hers. He knew how heavy the bonds of those chains were, and the only thing he'd succeeded in doing tonight was looping them around *her* too.

So he would give her the only thing he could give her. He would give her freedom. Even if she hated him for it.

'Get out,' he commanded, unconsciously echoing the words he'd said to her six months ago. 'Leave.'

He closed his eyes against the hurt he could see in her own.

'You're right,' he said, shaking his head. 'I don't need you. I don't need anyone. Our marriage will be annulled. We will be divorced. Whatever it takes. I'll be free to make a marriage with someone who understands what it takes to be a queen. Someone who can bring something to Farrehed other than selfish demands of love.'

He hated himself more and more. Every word dripped poison into his veins and hers. Every word was designed to make her leave. Every word—as hateful as they were—was a way for him to love her. To protect her from a life that would surely be her undoing.

Her face drained of colour and her eyes glittered in the dim lighting of the room. But still she remained determined.

He couldn't take another word falling from that lovely mouth of hers. He didn't think he would survive it.

'Get out!' he roared.

CHAPTER TWELVE

August 2nd, 07.00-08.00, Farrehed Embassy

THE BEAT OF Odir's pulse pounded within his head. Ripples shivered over his skin, through his body, over his mind and covered his heart. He was alone. Eloise had left. He didn't remember seeing her go. She must have slipped out while he'd had his eyes closed.

The banging came again, and Odir wondered if it wasn't his pulse after all. He didn't want to see anyone. Not like this. The pain he was feeling was nothing like he'd ever felt before. If this was what love was then he'd been right to avoid it for so long. He felt it like a punch to his gut, stealing his breath and causing agony to radiate around his body. Shock. He thought he might actually be in shock.

The banging came once more and finally, without waiting for his approval, the door swung open into the room and Jarhan stormed in.

'Where is Eloise?' he demanded.

Odir almost laughed. His brother had not spoken to him in such a way since they were teenagers.

'Gone.'

That one simple word finally put a name to the thing that had happened. That *he'd* made happen.

'Gone?' his brother queried.

'Gone.'

'Is that all you can say? What the hell happened?' Jarhan asked, casting his gaze around the room.

He stalked towards Odir in one easy movement and grabbed him by the shirt.

'What did you do to her?' he demanded, but the fury in his eyes was nothing compared to what Odir was feeling at that moment.

It struck Odir that just hours ago he would have taken his brother's behaviour to be jealousy, but it wasn't. It was love. Where yesterday he would have seen the lack of it, the absence of it as something that satisfied him, he now saw it all around him.

Jarhan's features changed at Odir's lack of response. 'You do know that nothing happened—?'

Odir seized the change in their conversation as a distraction, to protect his mind and his heart from thoughts of Eloise. Instead, he dragged forth feelings and emotions about his brother—reactions and thoughts he'd kept at bay for hours now.

'Why did you not tell me? I would have been there for you, Jarhan. I would have helped you in any way I could.'

Incredulity and anger shone in his words and Odir didn't care—he didn't care that his words betrayed his feelings. If tonight had shown him anything, it was that secrets and lies only destroyed.

'What could you have done?' his brother asked, removing his hands from Odir's shirt and shrugging in a helpless way that broke his heart even more. 'Would you have told the people of Farrehed? Would you have told our *father*? Torn our country apart because of your loyalty to me? Or would you have been forced to ask me to keep it a secret? To ask me to be something I am not?' Jarhan stepped away and turned his back to Odir. 'I could never put you in that position.'

'Because you didn't trust me to make the right decision?' Odir asked, terrified of his brother's answer.

'No,' Jarhan said, turning back to face him. 'Not at all. I *know* what decision you would have made. You would have stood by me and watched our country burn. Watched everything you had ever wanted for Farrehed go up in smoke because you love me.'

And there it was—simply said and simply accepted. This love that Odir had fought so hard against ever since the loss of his mother, ever since the change in his father. Despite all that had befallen them, his younger brother had not been tainted with that same despair.

'There may be a time in the future,' Jarhan continued, 'when what I am—*who* I am—will be ac-

cepted by our country. But not whilst our father sat
on the throne and certainly not right now. And that
is *my* sacrifice to make. That is *my* duty, *my* cross
to bear. Not yours.'

Odir threw a curse out into the room. He had been
so arrogant, so consumed with the need to protect
the people of Farrehed from his father's wilful ne-
glect, selfishness and paranoia, that he'd thought all
the weight of that duty had fallen solely on his shoulders. He hadn't even seen how his brother had made
his own sacrifices for duty, how he'd borne it on his
shoulders too. How strongly he'd carried it.

Odir forced his sluggish mind to work. To pick up
the threads of his earlier thoughts on how he would
shield his brother from the harsh realities of the im-
pact, of how this news would be taken by the people
of Farrehed.

'It'll not be easy, Jarhan. It'll not be accepted
fairly by the more traditional members of our society,' he warned. 'But I will be there if you want
to…to come out?' he said, struggling with the ter-
minology.

Jarhan's face cracked into a smile. 'Come out?'

'You know what I mean,' Odir said, feeling a faint
flush of awkwardness colour his cheeks.

It wasn't the subject that made it so, but talking
to his brother like this. They hadn't done it in years.
And it soothed him, it washed over just some of the
hurts of that day.

'Whatever your decision—and it is absolutely *your* decision—I'll be there. Standing beside you.' He pulled Jarhan into a hug. A hug that he took strength from.

'What happened with Eloise?' Jarhan asked from within the embrace.

'I let her go.'

'Because…?'

There were so many answers to that question. Because he couldn't willingly put her under the public microscope. Because he knew that his focus would have to be on Farrehed for the next few months. Because he couldn't abandon her as her mother had done. Because he couldn't use her as her father had done.

But beneath all that only one answer rang loud and true.

'Because I love her.'

Eloise rushed through the hallways, not knowing where she was going, not seeing where she was going through the tears falling from her eyes.

For six months, and even for years before that, she had never cried. She had kept everything inside, had focused on what needed to be done. For her mother, for Farrehed, for Jarhan, for Odir. And the first time she had asked something for herself, had wanted something just for *her*, she had been…*rejected*.

Her heart pounded in her chest. Pain ricocheted through her body. Agony. She was in agony.

She realised that no one was following her—not Odir, not one of his guards. She was no longer under his protection. She was truly alone, and that thought sent a jagged splinter through what was left of her heart.

She pushed through a plain doorway and found herself in a concrete stairwell. She made it down one half-flight of stairs before her foot, clad only in a silk stocking, slipped and she slid down the last step, tumbling into a heap in the corner of the stairwell.

The concrete around her was hard, cold and unforgiving. It bit into the bare skin of her arms and calves, drawing any warmth from her body and taking up the sounds of her cries, returning them again and again in an echo that must have reached both the heights and depths of the building.

Somewhere in her mind a thought rose. *This is the sound of a heart breaking.* And suddenly she didn't care that it was loud, undignified, that she was gasping for breath. She was in pain and she needed to let it out. It needed to be heard and recognised, not repressed and denied.

She was hurting, and there was something powerful in allowing herself to acknowledge that. It was evidence of how greatly she loved. So very different from her mother's repressed feelings, her father's tightly leashed control and Odir's denial.

She thought of each of them. She thought about how she'd let herself be used as a pawn in other people's games rather than standing up and saying no. She'd been passive, reactive, never really going after the thing that she wanted…until tonight.

She'd left Odir—but not because it was something that she wanted. She'd gone because of his command. For the first time she wondered whether, if Odir hadn't seen Jarhan kissing her she'd still be at the palace in Farrehed. Waiting for him to come to her. Filling her days with impossible tasks. Doing anything to make it right but the one thing that would have worked—talking, opening up, feeling and accepting her love for him.

Zurich might have been a moment of escapism for her and she'd never regret it. Not for one second. But despite all outward appearances it had been safe. Safe because it hadn't been something she'd wanted, but something she'd been forced to do. Yes, it had helped Natalia, and she'd be grateful for that for ever, but without Odir she'd have never reached out to Natalia. Even today she'd only come to London because she'd received his invitation to the event.

Today was her birthday. Today was the day she would inherit her grandfather's trust fund. She could still claim that money. It would keep her in Zurich, it would help pay for Natalia's treatment and she could go back to her secretarial role. But was that really what she wanted? To work day in and day out, claim her pay cheque, return to her little one-bedroom flat in Zurich. Eat dinner alone. Be alone.

She had come to the charity gala ready to ask for a divorce, ready to sever her ties with Odir, but he had shown her tonight that she had not been living at all in the last six months. She had simply been going through the motions. In just a few hours he had brought her to life. He had shown her the kind of passion that she was capable of. And, despite his bribery and lies, she had made the decision to help Farrehed, to put Farrehed first, and that had shown what kind of Queen she could be. One who was perhaps an equal to their King.

Thoughts clouded her mind, and the band of pain that had pressed in around her heart now wrapped itself around her head. She had told him that she loved him. And he had pushed her away.

She clutched her temples and groaned out loud in pain.

He had said that he wanted to be free to marry someone else.

The image of him standing before the world with a faceless bride, pledging to honour, protect and... and *love* her nearly killed her. But something about that image was off.

She knew Farrehed—she knew the people, their traditions and customs. They wouldn't be so easily accepting of a second marriage. And she knew Odir. He wouldn't risk causing upset—especially so soon after his father's death. His every action in the last twelve hours had been about ensuring the secure future of his country. So why would he risk that? Why would he do that now?

He had not said that he didn't love her. Only that he wasn't capable of it. And she understood why he thought that. Understood the damage done by his mother's death and his father's horrifying grief-stricken behaviour. But she knew it wasn't true. She had seen his ability to love in his every action towards Farrehed, had seen it shine from him when he had taken Jarhan into that hug when they had first come to the embassy. And she had seen it in his eyes when he had told her she looked magnificent.

Was it possible that he had let her go to *protect* her? Was it possible that this proud, sometimes arrogant and always powerful man had let her go for her *own* sake? Had he put *her* above the people that he loved so much?

'Running away again?'

Odir's voice from the balcony at Heron Tower only hours before echoed in her mind.

Perhaps she had been running. Yes, she had demanded love. But she had run at the first sign of trouble. Yes, she had been selfish—as he'd accused her. But that selfishness didn't make her feel ashamed. She had a right to demand love. But she hadn't stayed and fought for it. This time, rather than being scared, wanting to run away, she wanted to stand and fight.

This time she wasn't running away from something. She was running *to* it.

* * *

Eloise ran back through hallways that should have been full of people and activity but were strangely silent. She threw open the door to the royal suites but they too were empty. She flew down the steps towards the reception rooms, down the impressive circular stairway, and turned the corner to find...

Forty people staring back at her.

In the centre of the crowd were Jarhan and Odir, locked in conversation. It was only the ragged sound of her breathing that drew their attention—that and the sudden silence of the crowd around them.

Eloise saw shock register in Odir's face just before the royal mask came down and shut away his reaction. *Hope.* It left her with hope.

She took the next few steps down into the reception hall and barely registered the sound of forty voices resuming their chatter. People were shouting to each other across the room, and she could hear the buzz from the paparazzi outside the front doors to the embassy.

Jarhan broke away from the centre of the crowd, stalking towards her, and took her into his strong embrace.

'You've got three minutes—make them count,' he whispered into her ear.

And with that he disappeared into the crowd.

If she had expected people to part like the waves before their Queen she'd been wrong. She pushed through the crowd—against the tightly packed bodies that had formed a wall around her husband. Seeing her struggle against the press of people, Odir started making his way towards her, something like grim exasperation painting his features.

'Eloise, what—?'

'No,' she said, the moment he stood before her. 'You don't get to talk now. You don't get to issue commands or demand my removal from your presence. It's *my* time now, Odir. It's my time to talk.'

He pursed his lips together, wariness in his eyes now. Perhaps he was shocked by this new Eloise, she thought. Well, he'd better get used to it.

'This whole time I've been reacting to other people's demands—doing what was asked of me or doing what was needed of me. But I've never really done something for *me*. Not until tonight. Not until I wanted you to say that you love me. But you're right, Odir. I ran. I ran away from everything. You, my father, my mother. I spent six months hiding. And when I did come to fight for what I wanted—*you*—I stumbled at the first hurdle. I wanted you to tell me that you loved me. I wanted you to prove that you loved me. But I never proved that *I* love *you*.'

His eyes widened, and she knew that she'd hit close to home. It gave her the strength to continue.

'No one has ever shown you that you are worthy of their love and trust. Not your family, not your father, nor even your brother. I'm ready to place my trust and love in you. I know you love me. I know because you would never have sacrificed the future of your rule for me unless you loved me.'

He grasped her by the arm, pulling her closer to him, and in a rough, low voice he said, 'I *do* love you, damn it! That's why I let you go. I could never bind you to this life. A life where I will need to make sacrifices, where you will never be free from public scrutiny. There will be political manipulations for our whole lives, and I would not force that on anyone—especially not you. You've been so horribly used and manipulated by those who should have loved you unconditionally and I won't do the same. I could *never* ask that of you.'

There was a pain and hopelessness in his eyes the like of which she'd never seen before. But through it she could see the truth in his words, the truth in his heart, and her own heart soared.

'This is my sacrifice to make for the man I love. Because you have made me strong enough to bear it. I *want* this. I *choose* this. I choose *you*. I will stand by you and love you and be loved in return. All you have to do is say yes.'

Somewhere behind her a voice broke through the noise of the crowd.

'We go live in five…'

'Just say *yes*, Odir?' she asked.

'Four…'

'It's as easy as breathing.'

'Three…'

His finger reached up to wipe away the trace of a tear that had appeared at the corner of her eye.

'Two…'

The doors swung open on the front steps of the embassy, where the international press was waiting and the flashbulbs of the paparazzi exploded in front of them.

'Yes.'

'Ladies and gentlemen of the press, Sheikh Odir Farouk Al Arkrin of Farrehed and his wife have an announcement to make…'

EPILOGUE

Three years later, the Farrehed Embassy, London

THE SHEIKH OF FARREHED and his wife chased down the rich red carpeted halls of the Farrehed Embassy after a giggling, determined two-year-old hell-bent on freedom.

'Your child has inherited your waywardness, Wife,' complained Odir.

'And *your* stubbornness, Husband,' Eloise replied with a smile, slightly out of breath. 'I am too far gone for this, Odir,' she replied, stopping to lean against the cool walls of the embassy.

Glancing down, she placed a comforting hand over her seven-month pregnancy bump.

Odir checked the end of the hallway, seeing Jarhan scoop up his nephew, grin knowingly at Odir and head off, leaving a trail of tiny hysterical giggles.

'One day I fear that my brother will tickle our son to death.'

'Don't be silly. Besides, it's good to have someone to help out. God knows we'll need it when this one comes along.'

'Are you sure you don't want to reconsider hiring a full-time nanny?' Odir asked.

He understood his wife's reluctance, but still feared that two children would exhaust her.

'Absolutely. Besides, Mum has offered to come and stay—and Natalia's also on hand if we need her. Though I think she might have her *own* hands full soon enough.'

Shock registered in her husband's features. 'Really?'

'Really. But my lips are firmly sealed,' she replied playfully.

'More secrets, Wife?' he said, without a trace of the bite with which he had once spoken to her.

Eloise marvelled at how dramatically their lives had changed in three short years.

Despite her doubts, her mother had been telling her the truth that night almost three years ago to the day. Angelina Harris *had* sought the help she'd needed, but she had done it on her own terms, and Eloise wouldn't have wanted it any other way.

Her father had been deeply shocked two years before, when Angelina had served him with divorce papers and simultaneously—and very publicly—ended his political career.

Eloise and Odir had weathered the storm of family revelations, and the press had quickly lost interest once some other international scandal had taken its place. Two years on, Eloise and her mother had managed to carve out the tentative foundations of what Eloise hoped would be a strong, loving and honest relationship. It wasn't easy, but it was something that both women worked at each time they came together.

Natalia had also worked hard to overcome her personal demons and had undergone a successful transplant almost a year ago.

She felt a jerk in her stomach and groaned out loud.

'What's wrong?' Odir asked, concern building in his eyes in a second.

She laughed. 'Nothing. Just hiccups.' She took his hand and laid his palm over her stomach. 'I think it was all that running.'

Odir's hand jumped as another hiccup vibrated through her frame. And love, so pure and so strong, filled his gaze.

'Have I told you how much I love you?' he asked.

'Only yesterday. And the day before that. And the day before that. And all the days—'

Odir smothered his wife's response with the kind of passion-fuelled kiss he knew his wife craved more than any of the bizarre food she had desired during this pregnancy.

She pulled away from his kiss, leaning her head against the wall, eyeing him with a seriousness he had not seen for some time.

'Odir, I have a confession to make.'

His stomach clenched as he waited for his wife to continue.

'I have been keeping a secret from you.'

He waited, knowing that whatever she felt her secret was they would survive it, they would face it together. For there was nothing his amazing wife couldn't tell him. Nothing that would make him feel anything other than love for her.

'It's a girl.'

The smile that lit his wife's eyes wrapped itself around his heart, and in that moment Odir honestly couldn't want for anything more.

He leaned in close to his wife's ear and whispered his love for her over and over again. His heart only settled when she turned and told him the same. Truth and love was all they had ever needed and all they ever would.

* * * * *

Look out for more
Pippa Roscoe stories—
coming soon!

#3621 DESERT PRINCE'S STOLEN BRIDE
Conveniently Wed!
by Kate Hewitt

To reclaim his country, Zayed *must* wed. He steals away his intended...only to realize shy Olivia is the wrong woman! But with such heated chemistry between them, do they want to correct their mistake?

#3622 HIRED TO WEAR THE SHEIKH'S RING
by Rachael Thomas

As Jafar's temporary wife, Tiffany is perfect. Yet this convenient arrangement for his crown leads to passion! Is their craving enough to make Tiffany more than just the sheikh's hired bride?

#3623 SURRENDER TO THE RUTHLESS BILLIONAIRE
by Louise Fuller

Luis is shocked to learn the beautiful stranger he spent one scorching night with has also been hired by his family! He whisks Cristina away to uncover her ulterior motive...and rekindles their incendiary desire!

#3624 PRINCESS'S PREGNANCY SECRET
One Night With Consequences
by Natalie Anderson

Damon can't resist a sensual encounter with a captivating guest at a royal masquerade. But he's shocked to discover she was actually Princess Eleni—and now she's carrying his baby!

YOU CAN FIND MORE INFORMATION ON UPCOMING HARLEQUIN® TITLES, FREE EXCERPTS AND MORE AT WWW.HARLEQUIN.COM.

HPCNM0418RB

Get 2 Free Books,
Plus 2 Free Gifts—
just for trying the Reader Service!

"Did you forget to tell me about my baby?"

*Buttoned-up PA Cecelia Andrews's resignation
released her secret raw desire for her demanding
playboy boss, Luka Kargas. Now, one year after his
callous dismissal, Cecelia's hiding an even greater
secret—their daughter! She'll never let coldhearted
Luka make her daughter feel unwanted. But when
Luka uncovers her deceit, there's no escaping the
consequences of her passionate surrender...*

Read on for a sneak preview of
Carol Marinelli's *next story*
CLAIMING HIS HIDDEN HEIR
part of the **SECRET HEIRS OF BILLIONAIRES** *miniseries.*

"We were so hot, Cecelia, and we could have been
good, but you chose to walk away. You left. And then
you denied me the knowledge of my child and I hate you
for that." And then, when she'd already gotten the dark
message, he gave it a second coat and painted it black. "I
absolutely hate you."

"No mixed messages, then?" She somehow managed
a quip but there was nothing that could lighten this
moment.

"Not one. Let me make things very clear. I am not
taking you to Greece to get to know you better or to see
if there is any chance for us, because there isn't. I want

no further part of you. The fact is, you are my daughter's mother and she is too young to be apart from you. That won't be the case in the near future."

"How near?"

Fear licked the sides of her heart.

"I don't know." He shrugged. "I know nothing about babies, save what I have found out today. But I learn fast," he said, "and I will employ only the best, so very soon, during my access times, Pandora and I will do just fine without you."

"Luka, please…" She could not stand the thought of being away from Pandora and she was spinning at the thought of taking her daughter to Greece, but Luka was done.

"I'm going, Cecelia," Luka said. "I have nothing left to say to you."

That wasn't quite true, for he had one question.

"Did you know you were pregnant when you left?" Luka asked.

"I had an idea…"

"The truth, Cecelia."

And she ached now for the days when he had been less on guard and had called her Cece, even though it had grated so much at the time.

And now it was time to be honest and admit she had known she was pregnant when she had left. "Yes."

Don't miss
CLAIMING HIS HIDDEN HEIR
available May 2018 wherever
Harlequin Presents® books and ebooks are sold.

www.Harlequin.com